Too Many Secrets

Patricia H. Rushford

Jennie McGrady Mystery Series

1. Too Many Secrets
2. Silent Witness
3. Pursued
4. Deceived
5. Without a Trace
6. Dying to Win
7. Betrayed

Too Many Secrets

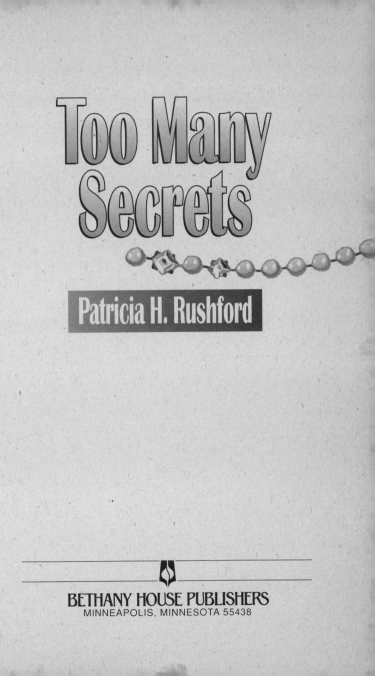

Patricia H. Rushford

BETHANY HOUSE PUBLISHERS
MINNEAPOLIS, MINNESOTA 55438

TOO MANY SECRETS
Patricia Rushford

Cover illustration by Andrea Jorgenson

Post-it is a registered trademark of 3-M Corporation for their
adhesive note paper.
Levis is a registered trademark of Levi Strauss for their
blue jeans.

Library of Congress Catalog Card Number 93–72042

ISBN 1–55661–331–8

Published by Bethany House Publishers
A Ministry of Bethany Fellowship, Inc.
11300 Hampshire Avenue South,
Minneapolis, Minnesota 55438

Printed in the United States of America

PATRICIA RUSHFORD is an award-winning writer, speaker, and teacher who has published fourteen books and numerous articles, including *What Kids Need Most in a Mom* and her first young adult novel, *Kristen's Choice*. She is a registered nurse and has a masters in counseling from Western Evangelical Seminary where she works as Writer in Residence. She and her husband, Ron, live in Washington state and have two grown children, six grandchildren, and lots of nephews and nieces.

Pat has been reading mysteries for as long as she can remember and is delighted to be writing a series of her own. She is a member of Mystery Writers of America, Society of Children's Book Writers and Illustrators, and Director of the Oregon Association of Christian Writers conference.

1

"Yes!" Jennie cheered and punched the air. Snapping the pages of her history text together, she tossed it on the book pile that littered her bedroom floor. Her good mood was not because Jennie loved history—well she did, but not that much. Actually, it was because she had finished her term paper. And that put her one step closer to a summer vacation with Gram.

Jennie eyed the half-packed suitcase in the corner. Not that she was excited or anything. She'd started packing a month ago, when her grandmother had given her a round-trip ticket to Florida for her sixteenth birthday. In exactly twenty-two days, Jennie would be roasting her pale Oregon skin in the Florida sun.

The doorbell rang. Jennie tore out of her room and hit the steps running. Probably Gram. The chimes rang again as she yanked open the door.

"Oh, hi, Aunt Kate. You're early." Jennie glanced over her aunt's shoulder into the gray drizzle. "Where's Gram . . . and Lisa?"

"Hi, Jennie, nice to see you too." Aunt Kate pulled her into a soppy hug and kissed her cheek. "Gram hasn't come in yet." She peeled off her dripping hat and raincoat and hung them on Jennie's arm.

9

Do I look like a coat rack? Jennie started to ask, but didn't. Probably because she did resemble a coat rack. Tall, thin, and shapeless. Which might explain why she was usually free on weekends.

"It's wet out there."

Jennie shrugged. *It's May. We live in Portland.* She opened her mouth to make the sarcastic remark, but that was as far as she got.

"Your cousin's at the club playing tennis with Brad. You know Brad, don't you?"

Jennie nodded. Of course she knew Brad. Lisa had been dating him for the last three months.

"Anyway, Lisa will be here in time for dinner. Be a dear and hang these up." She started down the hall. "Where's your mom?"

"In the kitchen." Jennie dumped Kate's clothes on a real coat rack and tagged along, wondering what kind of crisis her aunt was having this time. Not that Jennie was psychic or anything. It's just that when Aunt Kate got stressed, she also got spacey—hopping from one subject to the next like a bird trying to find a place to land.

Jennie followed her as far as the kitchen and leaned against the door frame, where she could watch and listen without being noticed.

"Got anything to drink?" Kate reached into the refrigerator, extracted a diet cola, and turned to Jennie's mom. "Susan, have you seen Gram?" Gram was actually Kate's mother, but everyone called her Gram. It was easier that way.

"Nope." Mom looked up from the clown cake she was frosting for Nick—Jennie's little brother. They were celebrating his fifth birthday that night. "Should I have?"

Kate shrugged and took a drink. "I'm worried. She

was due back from Canada two days ago. She hasn't called. And I can't reach her—she forgot to tell us where she was staying."

"So what else is new? You and I both know she didn't *forget*. She's being secretive again." Mom stepped away from the cake and scrutinized the red balloons she'd painted on the white frosting. "You know how she is. When she's writing, the world could come to an end, and she wouldn't notice."

"I know, but she promised to be back in time for Nick's birthday. She wouldn't forget that. You know how nuts she is about these kids." Kate inched a finger toward the cake.

"Hands off!" Mom's warning melted in a smile. "You're worse than the kids. You'll have to wait until tonight. And no, you can't lick the bowl—I already did."

"How about the spoon?"

Mom eyed the frosting-coated spoon lying on the counter with longing, then picked it up and handed it to Aunt Kate. "Ah," she sighed dramatically, "the sacrifices I make for my family."

"You really don't know where Gram is?" Jennie pushed away from the wall, irritated by their lack of concern.

They looked at her as though she'd just committed the social blunder of the century for interrupting their conversation. Jennie didn't apologize. It wasn't her fault they had been too engrossed to notice her.

"It's nothing for you to be worried about, Jennie." Mom wiped her hands on a towel and flicked the limp auburn bangs off her forehead. "You know the McGrady side of the family has always been a little . . . um . . . eccentric—especially Gram."

11

"Mmmm. Good choice of words, Susan." Aunt Kate licked another glob of gooey white frosting off the spoon. *"Ec . . . cen . . . tric."* Kate stretched it out, using a British accent and making it sound as if she were describing royalty. "I like that. Much better than loony-tunes or weird. I even like it better than *artistic.*"

"Maybe I should have said peculiar or bizarre," Mom countered.

Jennie half-listened to them throw adjectives at each other to describe the McGrady side of the family. Mom was right, in a way. There were some unusual things about their family. Such as Lisa and Jennie being cousins *and* best friends. And Uncle Kevin being Aunt Kate's husband *and* Mom's brother. Which explained why Jennie resembled Aunt Kate and Lisa looked more like Jennie's mom.

Ian McGrady, her grandfather, had been with British Intelligence in the Second World War and was killed ten years ago, in Lebanon, when terrorists blew up the hotel where he was staying.

Gram was supposed to be retired. She used to be a policewoman, but said it wasn't challenging enough. She quit the force after Grandpa died and moved to the coast. Gram was always off on some exotic assignment, writing for travel magazines and investigating some political or environmental issue.

Aunt Kate, who was Dad's twin, worked as a professional artist. Not that being an artist was all that weird. It's just that the way she combined colors and shapes it seemed she'd never heard of the word "normal."

Jason McGrady, Jennie's dad, was a pilot. He'd been working on a project for the government when his plane went down. A wave of panic rose and crashed inside her.

"What if Gram's plane . . ." Jennie stopped, realizing she'd said it out loud. Mom and Kate went white.

Jennie had a hunch they were remembering that day five years before, when the police told them Dad's plane had disappeared during a storm. He'd called in a distress signal to the Seattle airport, then lost contact. The authorities figured he'd flown off course and gone down in the Pacific Ocean. They never found him, and after a few months decided he must have died. Jennie didn't believe it. Dad was still alive—somewhere. She could feel it.

"I don't think we need to worry about the plane," Aunt Kate said. "She didn't take the Cessna this time. Flew up on Alaska Air. We'd have heard if anything happened."

"If Gram is missing," Jennie argued, "shouldn't you call the police or something?"

"Your mom is right, Jen. I'm probably overreacting. Besides, your grandmother can take care of herself. With all those self-defense classes she's taken over the years, I'd feel sorry for anyone who dared mess with her." Kate laughed, then sobered. "Still, she is nearly sixty . . . I'll call the Johnson's. Since Ryan picks up Gram's mail and does her yard work when she's gone, he may have heard from her."

The Johnsons were Gram's neighbors and their son, Ryan, was probably Jennie's best friend, next to Lisa. Thinking about Ryan brought another set of feelings— like the kind you get when you sit in front of a cozy fire on a cold rainy day. Ryan and Jennie hung around together whenever she visited Gram at the beach. He could be called a boyfriend, but only in the sense that he was a boy. Not that Jennie wouldn't have welcomed something more. Maybe she'd call Ryan later and ask him about

Gram herself. It couldn't hurt.

For the first time since Kate had entered the house, she landed. Perched on a swivel stool next to the wall phone, she flipped through the phone directory on the counter.

"Jennie." Mom's voice sounded strained. "It's okay to talk about your dad, you know." She put an arm around Jennie's shoulders and hugged her. "Talking helps us accept the fact that he's gone."

Jennie shrugged away. "I don't want to accept it. He's not gone. He's *missing*. In case you've forgotten, there is a rather large difference. They never found him or the plane, remember?"

Mom looked like she was about to argue, then stepped back. She glanced at the clock above the sink and sighed. "It's almost three-thirty. Would you pick up Nick while I finish getting things ready for his party?"

Her words implied the talk was over, but her eyes said, *We'll finish this later*. Jennie grabbed the keys to the Mustang from the hook next to the back door and paused, wanting to know what the Johnsons had to say about Gram.

Aunt Kate hung up the phone. "No answer. I'll try later."

The frown creasing her forehead told Jennie that Aunt Kate was more concerned about Gram than she wanted them to believe.

Jennie ran from the porch to the car, dodging raindrops the size of golf balls. She should have worn a jacket, or at least taken the umbrella. By the time she got into the car, her sweatshirt hung around her shoulders like a soggy towel. The freezing blast of cold air from the car heater forced the dampness into her bones. Jennie flipped the fan off and backed out of the driveway.

Despite the cold, she felt better. Jennie enjoyed driving. Mom had encouraged her to take Driver's Ed. and get her license right away. Mom liked having another driver in the house and treated Jennie like an adult—most of the time. They hardly ever argued. Lately, though, Mom had been acting weird—about a lot of things. Like that comment about Dad, for example. She used to get all weepy whenever his name came up. Hardly cried at all anymore. Not that Jennie wanted her to be sad. She just didn't want her to forget.

After Jennie had driven a couple of blocks, she turned the heater back on. Warm air currents beat against her skin, but inside, Jennie still felt the chill. If anything happened to Gram she wouldn't be able to . . . *no*. She wouldn't think about that. Gram would come. She would. "God, please," Jennie whispered, "please let her be okay."

She turned the radio on, hoping music would dispel her somber mood, but she got the news instead.

"Burglars escaped with over a million dollars in diamonds from the jewelry trade show at the Red Lion Inn last night," the newscaster reported. He went on to say they had no suspects in the case.

Jennie would have to remember to tell Gram about the diamond heist. Even though Gram didn't work on the police force anymore, she liked hearing about cases like that.

"Who do you think did it, Jennie," she'd ask. Then they'd try to solve the mystery. She hoped Gram would be back before the police figured it out.

As Trinity Center came into view, she shoved her thoughts about mysteries and Gram into a back corner of her mind. From the top of the hill, the blue metal roof reminded Jennie more of a headless peacock than a building. The church was in the middle, and the school fanned out from it. Nick's preschool was housed in the first section, the high school where Lisa and Jennie went was on the opposite side. The other grades fell in between.

Jennie turned into the long, steep driveway and parked at the curb near the preschool rooms and headed inside. When she walked in the door, Nick shot across the room and landed at her feet.

"Look what I made!" With one arm wound around her leg, he held up a mud-colored finger painting for her inspection.

Jennie pried him loose and knelt beside him. "Wow! What a great dog. I love his red and blue coat."

"It's not a dog, silly." Nick cocked his head and gave her his you're-not-very-bright look. "It's a horse. See, this is a tail and there's a saddle. He ain't got a rider cause he bucked him off."

"You're a really good artist," Jennie said. "I don't know how I could have made such a silly mistake." She hugged him and kissed the tip of his nose. "You better get your stuff so we can go home and get ready for your party." His eyes widened, and he galloped off to the coat racks.

"I can't get over how good you are with him." Nick's teacher appeared at Jennie's side.

Jennie shrugged. She'd had a lot of practice. "Nick's a great kid."

"You're not so bad yourself."

"Yeah . . . well . . . ah, thanks. We gotta run. Nice talking to you." She collected Nick and his masterpiece and backed away.

Jennie didn't talk much on the way home, just listened to Nick chatter about his day. He asked who'd be at the party, so she told him the guest list. It wasn't long, just family. Aunt Kate and Uncle Kevin, Lisa and her eleven-year-old brother, Kirk, and probably Lisa's boyfriend, Brad. Jennie hadn't mentioned Gram so Nick wouldn't be upset in case she couldn't come. Jennie hoped he wouldn't notice. She should have known better.

"What about Gram?" Nick twisted around in his seat and tucked his feet under him so he could see out the window. "Isn't Gram coming?"

"I'm not sure, Nick. She might not be home from Canada yet."

"But she promised."

"I know. She'll come if she can. I'll bet she's on her way right now." Jennie hoped she sounded more positive than she felt. The thought of Gram not showing up had given her a stomachache. Jennie tried to imagine Gram's candy-apple red antique T-Bird convertible parked in their driveway and Gram stepping out. She'd pull off her sunglasses and run a hand through her salt-and-pepper hair, trying to put her windblown curls in some kind of order. Then she'd smile and stretch out her arms, and Nick and Jennie would run into them. . . .

Jennie pulled into the driveway. Gram's car wasn't there. And it was still raining.

2

Get a grip, McGrady, Jennie told herself. *You're not going to cry.* She took a deep breath, switched off the ignition and reached for the door handle.

"Jennie." Nick's voice had dropped to a conspiratorial tone. "Do you think Dad will come?"

"Maybe." She swallowed back the lump in her throat. Nick had been born four months A.D. (After Dad), but he knew Dad almost as well as she and Mom. Nick didn't have memories, but he had pictures and stories. Dad's coming home was something the two of them thought about, especially on holidays and birthdays. They prayed a lot and for good measure, wished on birthday candles, turkey wishbones, and falling stars.

The wishes hadn't come true and neither had the prayers. Jennie looked out the side window, not wanting Nick to see the tears in her eyes or the doubt written on her face.

"Don't cry, Jennie." Nick touched her arm. "We're going to get a daddy. You'll see. In my prayers last night I asked God if I could have Daddy for my birthday and He said yes."

Oh, great. Jennie wiped her cheeks with her damp sweatshirt sleeve. She had that one coming. She'd built

18

Nick's hopes up—told him Dad would come home some-day. Now he'd be disappointed, and it was all her fault. Mom's fault too, Jennie reminded herself. It was Mom who always insisted on praying.

According to her, God heard everyone's prayers and answered them. Jennie remembered asking her, "If that's the case, why isn't Dad home yet?"

"God's answers aren't always what we want to hear," she had said, "but they are always right for us."

Jennie figured if God didn't think bringing Dad back home was right for them, then there was no point in pray-ing about it. She didn't want anything or anyone else. Just Dad. Well, Jennie wouldn't have to depend on wishes and prayers any longer. She had a plan.

By the time Jennie got around the car to help Nick out, she was smiling. "Let's go show Mom your beautiful horse."

"Should I tell her Dad's coming?"

"No, I think we should let it be our secret." The last thing Jennie wanted right then was for Mom to tell Nick that Dad was never coming back.

Nick giggled and raced into the house, down the hall, and into the kitchen. "Where's my cake?"

"Whoa, Tiger." Mom tackled him as he tore past her. "First the coat, then a hug for me, *then* you can see the cake."

Jennie folded her arms, leaned against the door frame and watched Mom wrestle Nick out of his little jacket. "Where's Aunt Kate?"

"Gone home to pick up Kevin and the kids. They'll be here in a couple of hours." Mom lifted Nick up so he could see his birthday cake.

"Jennie, come see. Mom made my cake with a clown

19

on it with balloons and everything."

Jennie joined them at the counter. "Looks great, Mom."

"Thanks."

Nick squirmed out of her grasp and scampered off to the family room to watch *Mr. Rogers* and *Sesame Street*.

"How about having a cup of tea with me?" Mom asked when he'd gone. "There's something I need to talk to you about."

Jennie didn't want to talk to her mother right then. She was probably going to continue the conversation she'd started earlier. "Can't. I'm soaked and I've got a ton of homework . . . maybe later."

For a minute Jennie thought she was going to insist, then she looked at Jennie all sadlike and sighed. "You do feel a bit damp. We'll talk later."

Jennie wasn't doing too well on the relationship thing at the moment. Mom was probably thinking she'd suddenly gone rebellious on her. Jennie hadn't. Not really. She just couldn't handle Mom talking about Dad being gone for good.

Once she got to her room, Jennie locked herself in, yanked off the damp sweats, threw on her pink terry robe, grabbed the phone and dialed Gram's number. When she didn't get an answer, she called Ryan. No one answered there either. After she hung up, something nagged at her, felt out of place, but she couldn't think what and shrugged the feeling aside.

Mom and Kate were probably right. Maybe she was getting all worked up over nothing. But Jennie had good reason to be worried. Without Gram her whole summer would be ruined. It wasn't just the trip to Florida; she'd be disappointed if that fell through, of course, but there was something else. Jennie needed Gram's police training and investigative skills to help her find Dad.

Jennie's plan, the one she hadn't told anyone about, not even Lisa, was to stay with Gram all summer and talk her into reopening the case. It wouldn't be hard. Jennie had the feeling Gram had already done some snooping on her own. It wasn't anything she said, just the look she'd get in her eyes, the trips she took, the secrets. Gram had a lot of secrets.

Jennie wished she could have talked with her mom about it. She'd tried once around Christmastime. Mom had looked up from her knitting and said, "Jennie, you're chasing rainbows. It's time to grow up and face reality. You can't find your father, no one can. He's dead." Mom had picked up a tissue and pretended to blow her nose.

In a way Jennie could understand how Mom felt. Five years was a long time to wait. But Dad was alive. He was out there somewhere, and somehow Jennie would find him.

Fortunately, Gram and Mom didn't think alike. Jennie remembered Gram telling her and Lisa stories when they were little about Noah and the ark and the rainbow God gave them when the flood ended. When she finished her stories she'd smile and say, "God gave us rainbows to remind us that He will always bring sunshine after a storm. Rainbows are a sign of hope to give us faith no matter how terrible life gets."

Gram would help her find Dad. *But Gram is missing. No! Don't even think it, McGrady. You have to think positive.* "Gram is coming." Jennie said the words aloud to drown out the negative voices in her head. Gram might have forgotten like Mom said. Or maybe she's on her way. Maybe she found Dad and is bringing him with her.

"Yeah, and maybe you'll sprout wings and fly," Jennie heard herself say. The sarcasm surprised her. What was wrong with her? She was usually positive about him being alive, but lately she'd been feeling more and more like a little girl playing make-believe. Part of her was so sure, yet another part of her kept saying, "It's no use."

Knowing what she had to do, Jennie yanked open the closet door and pulled down her journal and a large cardboard storage box labeled "Dad's Things" from the closet shelf. If she got to thinking he might not come back or forgot what he looked like, she'd look at his stuff and write him a letter.

Jennie set the box on her bed and reached for his picture—the one she kept on the nightstand. Dad's eyes were dark blue, the shade of new denims. He looked back at her as though they were sharing some kind of secret, and Jennie almost expected him to wink. She set his picture down, then plopped his tweed hat on her head and wrapped the matching wool scarf around her neck. Her friends would probably think she was a little strange, but somehow, wearing his things brought his memory closer. And Mr. Banks, her psychology teacher, would probably say, "Miss McGrady, you appear to be obsessing." But it wasn't like that. She just needed to think about him sometimes and talk to him.

"I'm sorry, Dad," Jennie whispered, then picked up her journal and pen and started writing.

Dear Dad,

Back in the car when Nick asked if you were coming home, I got really shook. It wasn't Nick's question that scared me, it was my reaction. For a minute, I had a terrible feeling you were never coming home. I'm sorry for doubting. I know you'd be here if you could.

Mom's comment about your never coming back must have set me off. But don't worry, I'm sure Mom didn't mean it. We won't forget you, Dad, and we won't give up. But please try to come back to us soon . . . and if you can't . . . maybe Gram and I can come to you.

Your faithful daughter

Jennie signed the letter and set the journal aside. Someday, when he came home, she would sit beside him and let him read it. She picked up his picture again and traced the outline of his face, his almost black hair. She and Nick had inherited their Dad's blue eyes and dark hair. Jennie had also inherited the McGrady shape—lean and lanky, just like Aunt Kate and Gram. She had her Mom's nose, but that was all. Lisa was shaped just like Jennie's mom, about five-three, with curves in all the right places. Kate kept telling Jennie not to worry. "We may never fill out a B-cup," she'd say, "but at least we won't have to worry about being overweight."

Jennie smiled. She liked being a McGrady, even down to the stubborn streak that her mom kept hoping she'd grow out of. Jennie took the rest of her dad's things out of the box, one by one. The wooden horse she'd given him for Christmas one year. His golf trophy from college. The model airplane they'd worked on together one winter when he was between assignments. The rocks and shells they'd collected on the beach by Gram's house. When they covered her comforter, she knelt on the floor, rested her arms on the bed, and stared at them for a long time.

"Jennie." Mom knocked on the bedroom door. "It's five o'clock. Hurry and get ready, then come help me with dinner. There's something I need to tell you before everyone gets here."

"Be there in a minute." Jennie returned Dad's things to the box and set them, along with the journal, on the closet shelf. It didn't take long to pull on jeans and a cotton sweater and check her hair. She stuffed her feet into a pair of loafers on her way down the stairs.

The doorbell rang as she reached the landing. "I'll get it," she yelled. "Maybe it's Gram." *And Dad.* She smiled at the thought.

"Me!" Nick squealed as he squeezed in front of her and pulled open the door. "Let me. Let me!"

"Hi, you must be Jennie." Jennie felt the smile slide off her face as a man in a leather bomber jacket stretched out his hand.

3

Jennie ignored the man's hand and stared at him. For a second she thought it might be Dad—but only for a second. This man's eyes were lighter, more like faded denim than indigo. His hair more brown than black.

"Ah . . . I'm Michael." When Jennie didn't answer, he lowered his hand and hunkered down in front of Nick. "And this must be the famous birthday boy." The stranger produced a bright red package with a polka-dot bow from behind his back.

"Michael . . ." Mom's voice sounded out of breath as she came up beside them. "You're early. Come in."

"Mom!" Nick beamed up at her. "Look what the man gived me. Can I open it now?"

"No, you cannot." Mom stooped to ruffle his hair. "You know the rules about presents. Put it in the living room with the others. You can open all of your presents after dinner." She straightened and shifted her gaze to Jennie.

"Ah . . . Jennie." She wiped her hands on her apron. "I meant to tell you before, but we got busy." She looped her arm around the stranger's and drew him into the house. "This is my . . . friend, Michael Rhodes. We met through the singles group I've been going to and we've

". . . ah . . . I invited him to Nick's party."

Jennie felt as if she'd been slugged in the stomach. It wasn't so much what Mom said, it was the way she looked at him. The way he looked at her. Jennie backed away, her stomach churning like a cement mixer.

"Why don't you get Michael a cup of coffee?" Mom smiled, but her eyes warned Jennie not to make a scene. She turned back to the man whose bulk nearly filled the doorway. "Let me take your jacket."

"In a minute." Michael wrapped his arms around Mom and kissed her. He drew back and chuckled. "I've been waiting all day to do that."

The pizza Jennie had eaten for lunch suddenly decided to escape. She ran to the bathroom, leaned over the toilet and heaved.

That was how Mom found her a few minutes later.

"Oh, honey, you're sick."

Brilliant observation, Jennie felt like saying, but didn't for fear she'd upchuck again.

Mom mopped her face with a warm washcloth. "Do you want to lie down for a while?"

Jennie nodded. With her mother's help she managed to get to her room and crawl into bed. Mom sat beside her on the bed and smoothed back her hair. "It's not the flu, is it?"

Jennie turned toward the wall and closed her eyes.

"I'm sorry, honey. I didn't mean for you to find out about Michael this way. I was going to tell you earlier, but . . ."

"Why?" The word came out in a sob.

"I care about Michael. We've decided to start dating and I thought . . ."

"How could you? What about Dad?"

"Your father is dead, Jennie. He isn't coming back. We can't go on pretending anymore. We need to get on with our lives. Why can't you accept that?"

"Don't say that! Don't ever say that!" Jennie turned onto her stomach and crammed her head under the pillow. "They never found him. They never even found the plane."

The doorbell sounded, and she heard voices in the entry. "All right." Jennie felt the bed shift as her mom stood. "We won't talk about it anymore tonight. Take a few minutes to wash up, then I want you downstairs. I won't let you spoil Nick's party or Michael's visit. Is that clear?"

Then you shouldn't have invited him, Jennie wanted to yell, but didn't. She just lay there waiting for her mom to leave. She felt as if some strange creature had taken over her body. She *never* got emotional. Lisa was the dramatic one. Jennie liked being calm and in control. And to throw up! How embarrassing. Just because Mom had a friend. A male friend. A very attractive male friend. Jennie groaned and rolled onto her back.

So Mom's dating a guy, Jennie told herself, trying to be rational about it. *So what? It's no big deal.*

It is a big deal, another part of her argued. *She has no right to get involved with another man. Not now, not when I'm so close.* Jennie had been waiting for years for this chance to travel with Gram . . . to talk her into helping find Dad. She'd rehearsed the scene a hundred times. Jennie and Gram would find him. Having lost his memory, he would be living alone, going out of his mind with worry, wondering who he was and whether or not he had a family. He'd see the two of them, and his memory would come back. They'd hug and kiss and take him home. The

McGradys would be a family again: Dad, Mom, Nick, and Jennie.

That is so stupid, McGrady, you're acting like a baby. Jennie shook her head to clear away the confusion. It didn't help. Her thoughts flew around like dust in a windstorm, then settled back in her mind again. Maybe she *was* acting like a child—maybe her dream was nothing more than a fairy tale. She was overreacting to Michael. Jennie knew that, but she couldn't help it. Michael Rhodes did not belong in their house or in their lives, not while there was a chance Dad could still be alive.

Jennie got out of bed. She had to think of a way to get Mom to stop dating him. First, though, she had to pull herself together and get through Nick's birthday party.

While Jennie waited for the splotches on her face to disappear, she straightened her room, then brushed and rebraided her hair. She was furious with Mom, but to be honest, she was even more upset with herself for being such a wimp.

"Jennie?" Lisa knocked and let herself in. "You okay? Your mom said you weren't feeling good."

"I'm fine. Is dinner ready?" Jennie wrapped a band around her thick braid and tossed it over her shoulder so it hung down the middle of her back.

"Yeah." Lisa cocked her head and frowned. Her mass of silky red curls swayed to one side, reminding Jennie of a model she'd seen on a magazine cover. Lisa's hair wasn't red exactly, more like copper—like a copper penny. "You know, I should be mad at you."

"Why?" Jennie walked past her and out of the room.

"For keeping Michael a secret. I thought we'd promised to tell each other everything."

Lisa nearly ran into her when Jennie spun around. "I didn't know, so how could I tell you?"

"You mean she's been dating that guy and didn't say anything?"

"That about sums it up."

"You must be pretty ticked." Lisa's green eyes met Jennie's.

"You could say that." The concern in her best friend's eyes settled her. Jennie turned around and started for the stairs. "I should have guessed, though. She's been acting different lately . . . happier, singing a lot. She's been going to that meeting at church on Wednesdays. I just thought she was having fun. I thought she loved Dad as much as I do . . . I guess I was wrong."

"I can't believe she didn't tell you."

"I think she was going to, but that still doesn't make it right." Before Lisa could ask any more about it, Jennie changed the subject. "Did your dad and Kirk come?"

"Yeah." Lisa gave Jennie a look that said she'd let the discussion about Michael and Mom go for now, but that it was far from being over. ". . . and I brought Brad. Everyone's here except Gram."

"Did she call?"

"No. Not us, anyway. Mrs. Johnson told Mom that Gram had called them this afternoon to say she's still in Calgary and doesn't know when she'll be back."

Uneasiness settled over Jennie like a heavy blanket. She dropped onto a step in the middle of the stairway. "Gram didn't say when she'd be home?"

"No. Weird, isn't it?" Lisa scrunched down beside her. "I mean, you'd think she'd have called us, or at least sent us a card. We're her family, after all."

"I don't like it. Do you think something might have happened to her?"

Lisa shrugged. "Mom isn't that worried yet. She did say she thought Gram was getting too old to be running all over the country. She wishes Gram would stop working so hard and act her age—maybe take up knitting or something."

Jennie smiled at the thought. "That'll be the day. Can you imagine Gram sitting still long enough to knit an afghan?"

"Not really." Lisa grinned and placed her hand on Jennie's arm. "She'll be okay. Maybe she didn't have time for more than one call. Maybe she plans on calling us tonight during Nick's party so she can talk to all of us."

"I hope you're right."

"Jennie! Lisa!" Mom called from the kitchen. "Dinner's ready."

As the girls entered the dining room, Jennie tried to leave her jumbled feelings behind, but they wouldn't stay. They hung over her head like storm clouds, ready to burst. And they almost did when she walked into the dining room and saw Michael sitting at the head of the table—in Dad's chair.

Jennie couldn't remember ever hating anyone before. But at that moment she hated Michael Rhodes, and hated her mother even more. She felt like a time bomb about to explode, and it wouldn't have taken much more to set her off.

Jennie wasn't sure how she did it, but she managed to act normal. If anyone had known how Jennie really felt, they'd have nominated her for an Oscar. She avoided Mom and Michael and concentrated on Nick and the others. It wasn't until after dinner that the dam holding back her anger began to crumble.

4

Lisa and Jennie cleared the table and began washing dishes. Mom came up behind them and squeezed their shoulders. "Thanks, girls. Jennie, I know this hasn't been easy for you. Once you get to know Michael, you'll like him as much as I do."

Jennie scraped the food off another plate. *I will never like Michael!* she wanted to scream. Instead, she took a deep breath and tried to act as if it didn't matter. She didn't want to fight with Mom in front of everyone, and especially not during Nick's party. "Why don't you go back in the living room with the others?" Jennie suggested. "Lisa and I will finish up in here and bring out the cake and stuff." The strength and sincerity of her tone surprised her. Maybe she should take up acting.

Jennie felt rotten. She hated lying and pretending to be something she wasn't. But she'd never had to deal with anything like this before. And Mom was wrong. She shouldn't have asked Michael to come. She shouldn't be seeing him.

Mom hugged Jennie and kissed her cheek. "That's sweet. Thanks, girls. It's nice to be waited on."

When she'd gone, Lisa leaned back against the

counter and looked up at Jennie. "You don't like him much, do you?"

"That's the understatement of the year."

"Well, I think he's nice. Not only that, he's gorgeous."

"I can't believe you're saying that! I don't care how great he looks or how nice he is, my mother is a *married woman*."

"Get real, Jen. What if your Dad never comes back?"

The look Jennie gave Lisa could have melted steel at thirty paces. Lisa just frowned and continued. "I know you don't want to hear this, but he might not. Remember Angie's dad?"

Angie was a friend who lived in the house next door to Lisa. Her dad had left when Angie was only three. They thought he had been kidnapped or something. Then a few years ago they found out that he had another wife and family—a whole other life. And he didn't want to have anything to do with Angie and her mom.

"My dad's not like that."

"Maybe not, but . . ."

"Sorry to interrupt, girls." Aunt Kate breezed into the kitchen and grabbed a towel. "Thought you could use some help. And I'm not talking about the dishes. Your mom told me that Michael showed up before she'd had a chance to talk to you. I told her it probably wouldn't have made much difference. Am I right?"

Jennie nodded wearily. She wasn't sure she wanted to talk about Michael anymore.

"So . . ." Kate set the glass she'd been drying in the cupboard and leaned against the counter. "Why don't you tell me about it?"

Maybe I should talk to her, Jennie thought. Since Gram wasn't here, the next best person to talk Mom out of dating Michael would be Aunt Kate. Jennie chewed on her lip, trying to put her thoughts into words. "I tried to tell Mom earlier," she began. "She shouldn't be seeing Michael or anyone else. What if Dad comes home? What if he . . ." The words collapsed in Jennie's throat and everything blurred.

Kate pulled Jennie into her arms. "I know this is hard for you. It's hard for all of us. I love him too, Jen, and miss him like crazy. Losing Jason was like losing a part of myself. Every day I pray he'll come back to us. We all love him, especially your mom. But there comes a time when we have to let go. Your mother is young. She needs to get on with her life. She needs a husband, and you kids need a father . . ."

Jennie pulled away. This couldn't be happening. How could Aunt Kate say those things? Dad wasn't dead. He couldn't be.

"But, you said . . . you said you knew he was alive. You told me you could feel him sometimes. You said that twins have some kind of ESP thing and you . . ."

"Oh, Jennie. I'm sorry. I never meant to mislead you. It's just that we all wanted so badly for him to come back. I probably imagined it."

"No, you didn't imagine it. I feel it too. So does Gram." The sad look in Kate's eyes drained Jennie of hope that her aunt would help. Kate was on Mom's side. And from the comments Lisa had made, Jennie wasn't sure she could count on her cousin, either. She'd have to fight this alone—at least until Gram came back.

Gram will understand. She'll talk some sense into everyone.

Lisa stuffed a tissue into Jennie's hand. "Please don't cry. We can go up to your room for a while if you want.

Our moms can take care of the cake and ice cream."

"I'm okay," Jennie sniffled. "It's just been a rough day." She'd call Gram again later. And if she wasn't there, Jennie would track her down. Jennie had some money saved and would even go to Canada if necessary. Her whole world was coming unraveled, and it looked as though Gram was the only one who could hold it together. Jennie just hoped Gram would get there before it was too late.

Lisa and Jennie finished up the dishes in silence, then took the cake, party favors, plates, and ice cream into the dining room. "Come on, everyone!" Lisa called. "Party time!"

Lisa tried to sound upbeat and happy, but Jennie knew she was still upset about what had happened in the kitchen. Before the others came in, Jennie leaned toward her and said, "Thanks."

"For what?"

"Caring."

Lisa smiled. "I'm glad you noticed." She bit her lower lip as if she wanted to say something but didn't.

"What?" Jennie tightened her grip on the backrest of one of the dining-room chairs.

"Well, I don't agree with you about Michael, at least not completely, but I think I understand. If it was my dad . . ."

Nick zoomed in and scrambled onto the chair Jennie was holding and put an end to their conversation. Even if she didn't agree, Lisa would support her. Knowing she could count on Lisa's friendship lifted Jennie's spirits, and she actually began to enjoy Nick's party.

They sang happy birthday and laughed at Nick's antics as he blew out the candles and practically fell into his pile of presents. Nick tore into a squishy, pillow-shaped package, which turned out to be a sleeping bag.

"That's from us!" Kirk jumped up and showed him how to crawl through, under, and around it. When the boys finally surfaced, Lisa and Brad nearly created a riot with a space-age squirt gun they'd brought for Nick.

Mom snapped some pictures then tried to put an end to the chaos. "Enough, enough. If you guys don't quiet down I'm going to eat all the cake and ice cream myself."

Jennie even laughed at that. Mom had been trying to lose what she called her baby fat (the fifteen pounds she'd gained when she was pregnant with Nick) for five years. Her public helpings of cake were about the size of a pea.

"Hey, you guys better listen to her," Kate hollered. "I've seen her wolf down a whole package of double almond fudge cookies in one sitting." After another round of giggles they sobered up, and Jennie handed Nick another present.

The package from Mom contained rainy-day crafts, some clothes, and one of those picture Bible storybooks for little kids. "Oh, Mom . . ." Nick clasped his hands. "Thank you." From the lights dancing in his eyes, you'd have thought she'd given him a trip to Disneyland.

Nick picked up another present. "This one's from my sister," he announced proudly. The kid was a Mickey Mouse freak, and Jennie had wrapped the present in Mickey paper with a matching bow. He folded back the paper and found three of his favorite mouse books. Nick jumped up and grabbed Jennie around the neck in a bear hug. "Oh, thank you. You're the bestest sister in the whole wide world." He climbed up in her lap. "Read 'em to me now. This one first." He placed *Fantasia* on top of the pile and opened it.

Mom told us to smile while she focused the camera and took another dozen pictures. "Nick," Mom said as she loaded another roll of film into the camera, "Jennie can read one of the stories before bedtime. You still have another present to open."

She picked up the bright red package with the polka-dot bow. "Don't you want to see what Michael brought you?"

Nick turned to look at Jennie as if he needed her permission. She nudged him forward. "Go ahead. Open it." He scrambled off her lap and tore off the wrap. Inside the box lay a black T-shirt with a big neon picture of Mickey Mouse on the front. Nick jumped up, pulled his shirt off, and shrugged into the new one. It was the quickest Jennie had ever seen him move. She laughed along with everyone else over his enthusiasm.

Michael and Jennie glanced at each other at the same time. He smiled, and for a second she smiled back. She hated to admit it, but he couldn't have picked out a better present for her little brother.

Jennie looked away feeling like a traitor. *He's the enemy*, she reminded herself. *He's just trying to impress us.* He was sure doing a good job of it.

Nick yanked at Jennie's sleeve and motioned for her to lean forward so he could tell her a secret. "See, Jennie," he whispered. "I tolded you God would send us a daddy."

Hurt, anger, and frustration raced through Jennie, but before she could protest, Nick picked up the books she'd given him and walked over to Michael. "Michael, would you read me a story and tuck me in when I haf'ta go to bed?"

"Sure, Sport. I'd like that, but . . ." He looked from Nick to Jennie and back again. "Maybe you'd better make sure it's okay with your sister. I think she was planning on reading these to you."

Of course it wasn't okay. Anybody with any brains could see that. "Go ahead," Jennie mumbled, shrugging her shoulders as if she could care less.

Seeing Nick and Michael together was the hardest hit Jennie had taken all day. She felt as if she'd been used for target practice by practically everyone in the family. Her stomach was twisted in knots, her head ached, and her eyes burned. She had to get out of there before she made a fool of herself by crying again. "I'm still not feeling too well," Jennie announced. "I think I'll pass on the cake and go to bed."

Jennie mumbled a quick good-night and started to leave. Uncle Kevin, sitting beside her, stood and held out his arms. "Let's have a hug before you go, Jennifer."

Uncle Kevin's hug nearly undid her. He was not only Mom's brother, but he'd been Dad's closest friend. They had both flown helicopters in Vietnam. But, like all the others, he was already treating Michael like a member of the family.

Your family treats every guest that way, a voice in her head reminded her. Jennie ignored it. Michael wasn't just anyone. He was her mother's boyfriend. After escaping from her uncle's bear hug and telling everyone good-night, Jennie raced up the stairs and into her room.

Once in bed, Jennie leaned against the pillows, grabbed the phone and dialed Gram's number.

"Hello . . ."

"Gram!" For a second Jennie thought Gram was home, but the voice went on to say, "I'm sorry I missed your call. Be a dear and leave your name, number, and a brief message after the beep, and I'll call as soon as I can."

Jennie waited for the beep and said, "Gram, it's Jennie. I need you. Please call me. It's urgent!"

She hung up and snuggled deeper into the pillows, pulling the comforter up to her neck. Something about the calls to Gram didn't feel right. She closed her eyes and tried to concentrate, replaying the calls in her head. After a couple of minutes, Jennie decided her imagination was probably working overtime, so she tried Ryan's number. He answered on the third ring.

"Hi. It's me . . . Jennie."

"Hey, I was just thinking about you."

"Really?" Jennie wondered if his thoughts about her were anything like the thoughts she'd been having about him lately. Probably not.

"Yeah. I found this great cave in the rocks this afternoon. Just the kind of place you'd like. Smells a little fishy, but it's dry and roomy. And no bats."

"Sounds neat."

"So when are you coming down?"

"Soon . . . I hope. Gram's invited me to go to Florida with her in June. We should have a few days to explore before I leave." Jennie twisted the cord around her fingers. "That is . . . if . . . I mean, when Gram comes back. Ah . . . that's why I called. I'm really worried about her."

"Listen, like my mom told Kate earlier, we got a call from her saying she was still up north. I'm sure she's fine."

"Maybe you're right, but it doesn't add up. She missed Nick's birthday and didn't even call."

"Maybe she tried earlier and couldn't get anyone."

"We have an answering machine." The uneasiness Jennie had felt earlier resurfaced. "I tried calling Gram a few minutes ago," she said. "Left a message on her machine." Jennie shivered under the toasty covers. "Ryan?

Does Gram still call you to get her phone messages?"

"Not anymore. A couple of months ago she got a new answering machine. Now she can dial in and get her own messages."

"There's no chance that you were over there earlier tonight and accidently left it off?"

"No. When I brought her mail in this morning the machine was on and the red light was blinking."

The slippery thought crept out of its hiding place and wrapped its tentacles around her. "So the answering machine is always on?"

"Yeah, unless someone's calling in, in which case the line would be busy. What's wrong, Jennie? What are you getting at?"

"When I called Gram earlier, the answering machine didn't pick up. When I called a few minutes ago, it was on. If you didn't turn off the machine, who did?"

5

"I'm sure there's an explanation," Ryan reassured. "Maybe the machine malfunctioned. Maybe there was a power outage."

"And maybe someone was in the house. What if she came home? What if she's sick? She could have fallen. I just thought of something terrible. What if she had a heart attack or stroke in the sauna?"

"Relax, the sauna door was wide open this morning."

"There, that proves someone was there. She always keeps the door closed."

"It proves nothing except that we had a bad windstorm last night."

"But . . ."

"Jennie, she's not home and I really doubt anyone has been there." Ryan sounded annoyed, but Jennie didn't care. He sighed and said, "I'll look around tomorrow and give you a call. Don't worry. I'm sure Gram is fine. She's probably relaxing in some luxury lodge in front of a roaring fire, eating popcorn and drinking hot chocolate with friends."

"I hope not. Gram's allergic to chocolate."

Ryan laughed. "Oh, yeah, I forgot. Well, herb tea then. At any rate, knowing Gram, I'll bet she's gotten so caught up in writing the article and taking photos that she's blocked everything else out."

"Maybe, but I still don't think she'd forget Nick's birthday."

"She's getting older, Jennie. Could be her memory's going."

"I doubt it, but I suppose it's possible. Aunt Kate thought she'd forgotten to tell us where she was staying in Canada." Jennie yawned and stretched under the covers.

"You sound tired. I'd better hang up and let you get to sleep. Anyway, I'll bet she'll call tomorrow."

"Hope you're right."

"I know I am. But I'll give the house a thorough search and call you. Okay?"

"Thanks, Ryan. I really need to find Gram, even if it's just to talk to her. Things are going a little crazy here."

"Hmmm. Then I wish you were here. We could go for a walk on the beach. The moon's bright tonight. Surf looks like one of those oil paintings where you can almost see through the waves."

"Sounds wonderful." *And romantic.* She didn't dare say the last part out loud. Ryan wasn't interested in her romantically. She and Ryan liked a lot of the same things—reading, writing, beachcombing, exploring. But they were just friends. He'd never even kissed her. Even so, Jennie let her imagination conjure up a picture of the two of them, hand in hand on the moonlit beach.

"Jennie? Are you still there?"

She smiled. "Uh, huh. I was just enjoying the beach scene you described."

"Good. Hold those thoughts and try not to worry. And . . . um . . . I'll call you tomorrow."

After hanging up, Jennie concentrated on visions of moonlight and imagined herself and Ryan watching the waves. She could almost hear the pounding surf. It almost erased the image of Mom kissing Michael. Almost stopped her from worrying about Gram. Almost.

———

Jennie awakened to the sound of birds chirping. A rose-colored morning reached through the slats of the ivory miniblinds. The red digital numbers on the radio alarm told her it was only five-thirty. Jennie didn't usually get up for another hour, so she untangled the mess of twisted sheets and snuggled back under the covers. After about ten minutes of trying to go back to sleep, she gave up, shrugged into her robe, and slipped down to the kitchen to fix a cup of peppermint tea. She brought it back upstairs and climbed onto her window seat.

Jennie loved her room, with all its angles and the sloped ceiling. Mom had one just like it on the other side of the house, and Nick had the little square one in the middle. Aunt Kate had helped her decorate it after Jennie showed her a picture of what she wanted from an *Ethan Allen* catalog. Aunt Kate had wanted to go with a more vivid color scheme, but Jennie insisted that the wild colors Kate had picked would have driven her crazy. They'd ended up with ivory lace and floral prints, with burgundy and forest green accents. Mom thought it had too many frills, but Jennie liked it—especially the cushiony window seats. She leaned against a pile of pillows and pulled up the blinds to watch the birds flit around in the maple tree. She sipped the warm tea and thought about the day before.

Maybe she was numb, or not quite awake, but yesterday's memories seemed almost as fuzzy as the patches of mist rising from the cool ground. For a few minutes Jennie wondered if it had all been a bad dream.

Too soon, the haziness in her head cleared. *My mother, Susan McGrady, wife of Jason McGrady, is dating a guy named Michael Rhodes.* Nick thought Michael was the answer to his prayers. Jennie shook her head. If Michael really was God's answer to Nick's prayer . . . No. God wouldn't be that cruel. Would He? God was going to answer her prayers for *her* dad. Not a substitute. Michael's coming was just a coincidence—a terrible coincidence.

If only Gram would call. Jennie needed to talk things over with her. But what if she was missing? What if she really was in trouble?

"I've got to find her," Jennie murmured to the fat koala bear that leaned against a ruffled pillow. She picked him up and rubbed her face against his soft fur.

"Jennie?" Mom tapped on the door. "Are you awake?"

"Be down in a minute."

She sat there a little longer, trying to get the misty morning feelings back. Unfortunately, her mood had gotten as cold as the tea, so she dragged herself out of the window, showered, dressed, and headed downstairs.

"How long will you be in school this morning?" Mom asked as she buttered Nick's toast.

"About two hours." Jennie mashed her poached eggs into the hashbrowns and reached for the salt and pepper. "I have an assignment to finish in chemistry lab today, and I need to pick up some books at the library. I should be home about ten."

"That's perfect," Mom said. "I have an appointment downtown at ten-thirty, so you'll need to run Nick to school."

Jennie nodded, thinking how weird it seemed to be having such a normal conversation after what had happened yesterday. Mom didn't mention Michael, so Jennie didn't either. Maybe Mom was having second thoughts.

At seven-thirty Jennie pulled up in front of Lisa's house.

"You okay?" Lisa asked in an out-of-breath voice as she tossed her books in the backseat and climbed in the front.

Jennie shrugged, waited for a car to go past, then eased onto the street. "I've been better. Did Gram call you guys last night?"

"No," Lisa said as she snapped her seat belt into place. "Mom was talking about calling the police and filing a missing person's report if she didn't hear from her today."

"Good idea. I talked to Ryan last night and he didn't seem too worried. I don't know, though. I just can't get over the feeling that something's wrong."

"You worry too much." Lisa pushed a stray curl off her forehead. "Remember last year when Gram went to Mexico and came back a week late?"

Jennie nodded. Did she *ever* remember! "I don't even like to think about it. Gram could have been killed."

"You don't still believe that story, do you?"

She did. They had all gone to pick Gram up at the airport. Gram was wearing one of those huge sombreros and a bright pink gauze dress with a floral print shawl. She had practically danced all the way down the concourse. Later at dinner she told them a wild story about a gang of drug dealers who had kidnapped her and held her prisoner on a marijuana plantation because they thought she was a federal narcotics agent.

"Well, do you?" Lisa asked again.

"Part of it. I still wonder if maybe the kidnapping wasn't a mistake—that maybe she really was an agent."

"Oh, yeah. I remember our talking about that. We were really heavy into those Mrs. Pollifax mysteries then. We thought maybe Gram was working for the FBI too. But we were only fifteen. You don't still believe that, do you?"

"Why shouldn't I? It makes perfect sense. I mean, why else would she go to Iran? Remember that? She didn't even write an article about that trip."

"Still," Lisa said, "Gram's too old to be a spy. Maybe when she was younger, but at her age? She probably made the whole thing up so she wouldn't have to admit that she'd lost track of time."

Jennie sighed. "Maybe. Then again, maybe not." As they pulled into the school parking lot, she told Lisa about Gram's answering machine.

Lisa shrugged. "It was probably a malfunction like Ryan said. Anyway, I've got to run. Wish me luck. I have a test in algebra."

"Are you sure you don't want me to pray?" Jennie asked. "Between Mr. Olsen's algebra tests and your love for math, you'll need a lot more than wishes."

"Thanks for the vote of confidence," Lisa muttered as she jumped out of the car, collected her books, and jogged toward the building.

Jennie grinned, thinking how much Gram and Aunt Kate and Lisa were alike—not in looks, but in personality—always in a hurry, as if they're running late even when they weren't. Jennie shook her head and retrieved her book bag and notebook, then headed across the parking lot. It sure was nice not to be taking Mr. Olsen's test with Lisa. Jennie had finished up that module two weeks ago. She still had some assignments to finish, but the hardest part was over.

Mom had transferred Jennie to Trinity at the beginning of seventh grade, after getting into a major battle over what she called "the public school system's inflexibility." Since Mom worked nearly full time as a bookkeeper, she wanted Jennie home to baby-sit Nick when she had to be gone. Jennie attended school for a couple of hours three days a week. The rest of the time she used a home-school program.

At first Jennie had hated it. Home school was so different from what everyone else was doing. Now she thought it was great. She liked being in the same school as Lisa, and Jennie loved the freedom. Since she worked at her own pace, she would finish her sophomore year two weeks earlier than kids taking regular classes.

As Jennie pushed open the office door, Mrs. Talbot's high-pitched voice brought her thoughts back to the present. "Hello, Jennie. I was just thinking about you. Coach Haskel left a message for you to call him about being on the girls' basketball team next year, and you need to set up a time to take your SATs." She went back to her desk to retrieve the notes. "Oh, and this letter came for you this morning."

"For me? Here?"

She handed Jennie two green memos and a square envelope. "Struck me funny too," Mrs. Talbot said as she squeezed into a chair and scooted up to her desk. "Especially since we don't give out students' names. Who's it from?"

Jennie glanced at the envelope. "I don't know. It doesn't have a return address." After signing the attendance register, she hurried out to the hall, slipped the memos into her notebook, and fingered the peach-colored envelope. The writing looked familiar. Her hands shook as she tore open the envelope and unfolded the card.

Dear Jennie:
    I'm sorry I haven't been able to call. If anything happens to me, I want you to have the bracelet we found last summer.

                        Love you,
                        Gram

Jennie felt as if she'd been plopped in the middle of a Nancy Drew mystery. First Gram didn't show up for Nick's birthday, then that business with her answering machine, and now this.

Maybe Gram *was* getting senile. Jennie frowned and rubbed her forehead. The bracelet, an antique she and Gram had found in a crawl space at the back of Gram's closet, was tucked away in Jennie's jewelry box. Gram had given it to her the day they'd found it.

What did she mean, "if anything happened to her"? What could happen? Jennie shoved the note into an inner compartment of her book bag and headed slowly down the empty hall. Her footsteps echoed on the linoleum-covered concrete floor. She concentrated on the sound so she wouldn't think too much about Gram—so she wouldn't get scared and panic.

After turning in her term paper for history, Jennie headed for the chemistry lab to do an analysis of Dr. Adam's mystery liquid. She had managed to stash Gram's note out of sight, but her mind kept dredging it up. Why would Gram write a note about a bracelet she already had? Was it a clue? A secret code?

The bad part about worrying over Gram and her

strange message was that it took Jennie three tries to discover that the yellowish substance was $CO(NH_2)_2$—urine. The good part was that even though the bunsen burner had turned her first analysis to charcoal, she hadn't blown up the lab.

Jennie went through the rest of the day in a daze, trying to figure out what had happened to Gram. After dropping Nick off at preschool, Jennie decided Gram was a secret agent for the FBI, working on a case—maybe one involving an old bracelet. By the time she got home, Jennie was convinced that Gram had been kidnapped by terrorists and they'd never see her again.

A phone call from Michael brought an end to Jennie's mind maze. She told him Mom wasn't home, and she didn't know when to expect her.

"Have her give me a call," he said. "And Jennie, tell her not to make dinner. I'd like to take you all out for pizza."

"I'll tell her," Jennie said as she tried to think of an excuse not to go. In the end, after Mom threatened to take away her driving privileges if she didn't go peacefully, they all piled into Michael's metallic gray BMW.

Jennie liked his car and wondered how nice she'd have to be to talk him into letting her drive it sometime. The minute the thought escaped, Jennie crushed it. Michael was the enemy; she needed to remember that.

They ordered a large combination pizza with no green peppers or anchovies. Not only did Jennie act like the perfect daughter, she managed not to throw it all up when Michael slid his arm around Mom and whispered something in her ear. Mom giggled and scooted away.

How embarrassing. They were acting like a couple of love-starved teenagers! As soon as they got into the house

Jennie made an excuse to get away from them. "Thanks for the pizza, Michael," she said with as much enthusiasm as a corpse. "I'd love to visit, but I've got to work on my algebra assignment."

Jennie half-expected Mom to insist she stay downstairs and play a game or something, but she didn't. She and Michael just said, "Good-night," and walked arm in arm into the living room. A chill shuddered through Jennie as she watched them. Her mom really cared about the guy. Jennie only hoped Gram would come and talk some sense into her before it was too late.

Jennie grabbed a can of diet cola from the fridge and headed upstairs. Once in her room, she put Michael and Mom out of her mind and tried to concentrate on the note Gram had sent. She cleared off a spot in the center of her desk, laid the note down and stared at it. "What is she trying to tell me, God?" Jennie whispered.

She picked the card up and examined it from all angles. It was just an ordinary note card, with a couple seashells on the front and a brief note inside. The postmark on the envelope indicated it had been mailed two days earlier from Lincoln City, just a few miles from Bay Village, where Gram lived.

Jennie blinked and read the postmark again as she reached for the phone. Ryan answered on the first ring. "When did your mom talk to Gram?"

"What?"

"When did Gram call you and where did she call from?

"I don't know. Why?"

"It could be important."

"Hang on a sec and I'll ask Mom." When he came back on the line he said, "Gram called about four o'clock.

Mom said she didn't say where she was calling from but figured it was from Calgary. Gram said she'd been delayed and didn't want us to worry. What's this all about?"

"You're not going to believe this," Jennie said, "but I'm holding a note that Gram mailed from Lincoln City on May twenty-fourth. That was two days ago." Jennie read the note to him. "If Gram called you from Canada yesterday, what was she doing in Lincoln City the day before? If she was in Lincoln City, she would have just gone home . . . unless. . . . Ryan, something terrible has happened to her, I just know it."

6

"All right," Ryan said as he cleared his throat. "Let's not panic. There's got to be a reasonable explanation."

"There's an explanation all right, but I'm not sure how reasonable it is. No one can be in two places at once. Either Gram's been home or she's still in Canada." Jennie picked up her diet cola and pulled the tab.

"Maybe she got as far as Lincoln City and had to go back."

"Without calling us? No way." Jennie flopped down on her bed and turned over on her stomach. "Besides, she told your mom she'd be in Canada a few more days."

"You're right. It doesn't make sense."

"I'm really scared, Ryan. What if Gram is in trouble? What if she's been kidnapped or something?"

"Tell you what. I'll make a run into town tomorrow. Maybe someone saw Gram at the post office when she mailed your letter. Could be that the letter was misplaced for a while. Maybe she sent it before she left for Canada."

"I can't stand this." Jennie jerked to her feet and paced. "I should be there. I could look around the house—see if anything is missing. I could talk to her friends . . ."

"There's no need. Sheriff Taylor and his deputy came

51

by this afternoon asking questions about Gram. Kate must have asked them to check things out."

"Did they find anything?"

"Nope. They figure she's still up north. I think they'll keep checking though—you know how Sheriff Taylor feels about your grandmother."

"I know." The sheriff and Gram had been good friends since she moved there. Jennie took a long drink and sighed. "What did they say about the answering machine?"

"I didn't tell them."

"Ryan, it might be important!"

"Sorry. You're right, that was a dumb move. I'll call them tomorrow, but I doubt it will make any difference. Should I tell them about the letter she sent you?"

"No," Jennie heard herself saying. "Gram sent me that note for a reason, and I don't want anyone to see it until I figure out what she's trying to tell me."

"Maybe she just doesn't want anyone to know where she is. She could have sent the note, then called us to confuse everyone."

A glimmer of light emerged from Jennie's dark, swirling thoughts. "No. For some reason she wants everyone to think she's still in Canada. But at the same time she must have wanted me to know where she really was. Do you think she wrote to me so we wouldn't be worried?"

"I don't know. This is like something out of a spy movie."

"I know. It sounds far out, but do you think she could be working undercover with the police or something? She was a detective before she retired."

They talked more about the possibility, and for the first time in two days Jennie began to relax. "If Gram is

working on a case, maybe we'd better not do any investigating on our own." Jennie thought about the note Gram
had written. "Maybe she's telling us not to interfere unless something happens."

"So you don't want me to talk to the sheriff about the
answering machine, or check out the post office?"

"I guess not. Not yet anyway. If she *is* working on a
case, I don't want to mess her up. Like my mom always
says, 'Things have a way of working themselves out if you
give them enough time.' Be sure to call me if you hear
anything."

After hanging up, Jennie stripped and slithered into
a flannel nightgown. When she'd gotten ready for bed,
she tiptoed down the hall and peered over the railing into
the living room. Michael was still there. The two of them
were huddled on the sofa watching television. An ache
started in Jennie's stomach and worked its way upward.

Mom's singing and the smell of bacon and cinnamon
rolls greeted Jennie the next morning when she came
down for breakfast. The sun poured into the kitchen,
chasing away the shadows. Jennie tore off a piece of the
warm sticky roll and stuffed it in her mouth. "Hmmm.
These are great, Mom. What's the occasion?"

"I felt domestic this morning," she said, hugging Jennie. "And Michael's coming over for breakfast later." Before Jennie could reply, Mom changed the subject. "I'm
glad you're up early. I was hoping to get a chance to talk
to you alone."

Jennie slathered butter and syrup over her pancakes
and crammed a forkful into her mouth.

"I know my dating Michael is difficult for you to accept, but now that you've gotten to know him a little, what do you think?"

I think he's a jerk. Because she wasn't in the mood to argue and because she wanted to live through breakfast, Jennie said, "He's okay, I guess. He has a nice car."

Mom must not have been listening because she said, "That's good." She sighed and gave Jennie a kind of dreamy look. "Last night he asked me to marry him."

Jennie choked on her pancake. When she was finally able to breathe again, she gasped, "M-marry him? What did you tell him?"

"I said I'd think about it." Mom calmly sat down next to Jennie and took a sip of her coffee.

"I can't believe you'd tell him that. You can't get married. You're still married to Dad." He hadn't been declared officially dead and wouldn't be for two more years.

Mom either didn't hear her or didn't want to. She rubbed her thumb over the teddy bears on her mug. "I'm so torn." She got up and poured herself another cup and sat down again. "I . . . I'm tired of waiting, Jennie. Gloria, my counselor, says I need to stop 'chasing ghosts. . . . '" Seeing the frown on Jennie's face, she stopped to explain. "Gloria says I need to bury the past and get on with my life." Her eyes filled with tears. "I loved your dad, honey. But Michael is sweet and caring. I just don't know what to do."

Jennie didn't know what to do either—or say. Everything had been going fine until her mother started seeing that counselor. Gloria was making a mess of things for everybody. "You know how you're always telling me not to rush into things. Maybe you should wait awhile. I mean . . . we don't even know him."

"I'm not exactly rushing. Michael and I have been

seeing each other for nearly two months." She paused at Jennie's raised eyebrows and smiled. "I guess that's not very long, is it? It just seems like we've known each other forever.

"Anyway, a couple of weeks ago, we realized our relationship had grown beyond the friendship stage. I'd been so lonely, and Michael makes me feel . . . I don't know, alive."

Does that mean Nick and I made you feel dead? Jennie had been lonely too, but she wasn't about to go out and find a substitute father.

"I wanted you to meet him earlier," Mom went on, "but I kept putting it off. I guess I was afraid of having to deal with everyone's reaction. Gloria got after me for that. Said I needed to be honest—with you—with the whole family. I should have told you about Michael right away. I am sorry. I've handled this badly."

Jennie didn't know what to say, so she concentrated on her food.

"It wouldn't have made any difference, would it, Jennie? You'd still be upset."

She was right about that, but Jennie didn't answer. Instead, she pushed away from the table and headed for the door.

"Come back here! You haven't finished breakfast. And I'm not finished talking."

"I'm not hungry. I've heard enough."

"Sit!"

For a split second, Jennie debated whether to keep walking. Unfortunately, her mother still had a tendency to use grounding to keep Jennie in line. She sighed and walked back to the table and sat down.

"I had hoped you'd be mature enough to understand.

Jennie, please! Don't make this any harder than it is."

"You're the one who's making it hard," Jennie snapped back. "You're the one who's being immature. You said you'd love Dad forever. You said marriage is supposed to last a lifetime. We were doing okay . . ."

"Your father is gone. He doesn't live here anymore, and we've got to stop pretending. Can't you see that?"

Jennie folded her arms tight across her chest and stared at a bacon crumb on the plate.

"And, we were not doing okay, Jennie. We've been miserable . . . I was miserable. When Pastor John suggested I see a counselor, I did. I've made some serious mistakes with you and Nick, letting you hold on to the hope that your father was alive. He isn't coming back. He's gone. I've accepted that and said goodbye. You need to say goodbye too."

"No!" Jennie wanted to get up and run. Or throw her dishes at the wall. Mom's words hung in the room like lead weights. "Why are you doing this? Why couldn't you leave things the way they were?" Jennie had barely finished the last sentence when something broke inside her. She pushed her palms tight against her eyes, but the tears squeezed out anyway.

Mom scooted her chair toward Jennie and patted her head. She always did that when Jennie was upset. It felt good being held by her again, like when she was little, but it made her cry even harder. Jennie didn't want to feel good. She didn't want to cry.

"Poor baby," her mother crooned. "It's going to be all right. We're going to be all right. Gloria said it would be hard at first, but once you talk to her . . ."

Jennie did move then—fast. She jerked to her feet and sent the milk and coffee flying. Mom jumped up, grabbed a towel, and started mopping the table. Jennie turned away from her and ran.

"Jennie! Get back here!"

Jennie stopped at the doorway and turned to face her mother. "No way! I'm not talking to some dumb shrink. You shouldn't be seeing her either. She's turning you against Daddy. She might have brainwashed you, but not me."

"Jennifer McGrady!" Mom yelled as Jennie ran out of the room. She caught up with her at the landing, grabbed her arm, and spun Jennie around. The strength in her mother's grip surprised her. "This attitude of yours has to stop, young lady. I love you, but I'm not going to allow you to run this family. I'd like nothing more than for you and Nick to accept and love Michael as much as I do. I'm willing to give you some time, but you need to know right now that if I decide to marry Michael, I'll do it with or without your approval."

Her grip loosened and Jennie pulled away. Her mother's words followed her up the stairs. "You have an appointment with Gloria on Monday afternoon. You *will* be there."

———

Over the weekend Jennie had taken Dad's things out three times and written him another letter. By the time Monday arrived, Jennie was ready to combat the shrink.

In the counseling office at church, Jennie talked to Gloria about school, how she loved taking care of Nick, and how well she and her mother usually got along. Since Mom had said that holding on to the hope her dad would come back was "unhealthy," Jennie first told Gloria that she missed her father. She even said she could understood how her mom felt—which was a lie, of course. Jennie didn't think she could ever understand how Mom could turn against Dad and even think about marrying Michael.

Jennie didn't mention her box full of Dad's things or the letters. She didn't tell her about the plan to find him this summer. She was afraid Gloria would declare her a nut case. Near the end of the session Gloria tilted her head and leaned forward. "Losing your father has been hard for you."

I haven't lost him, Jennie wanted to argue. *He's still alive, I know it.* Aloud she said, "I'm doing okay."

She smiled. "Yes, but from what your mother has told me, you both have some things to work out. I'd like to see you once a week for a while. We have several camps coming up this summer that are geared to help adolescents deal with grief issues."

"I'm spending the summer with my grandmother," Jennie said. The familiar ache began to spread through her again. *They wouldn't dare keep her from staying with Gram, would they? They'd better not,* Jennie decided. *If they try it, I'm leaving.*

"Your mother mentioned that, but I think we can still work some therapy in. In fact we have a camp beginning June first. We still have some spaces available. Why don't we sign you up?"

Jennie didn't like the idea of them talking about her, or making plans for her life, but she kept quiet.

By the time Jennie got out to the car, her hands were shaking so hard she could barely get the key into the lock. Something about the way Gloria had talked made her wonder if Mom would make her go to therapy instead of to Florida with Gram. She couldn't let that happen. Somehow in the next two weeks Jennie had to make them think she'd made a miraculous recovery. She'd go to the stupid camp if she had to—at least it would get her away from Mom and Michael for a week. By then Gram would be home for sure. They would go to Florida, and maybe Mom would forget about the counseling. Maybe, once Mom talked to Gram, she'd forget about Michael too.

Jennie hated lying, but she hated what her mother was doing even more. What else could she do? "Gram," Jennie whispered, "I don't know where you are or what you're doing, but please come home. I *need* you."

––––––––––

For the next couple of days Jennie almost stopped worrying. She had called the courthouse and discovered that as long as Mom was still legally married to Dad, she and Michael couldn't get married. Besides that, Mom had said she thought it was probably too soon to get married and that Nick and Jennie needed to get to know Michael better.

On Wednesday afternoon, Jennie let herself relax and even managed to have fun when Michael took her, Lisa, Kurt, and Nick to the amusement park. *I'm not selling out*, she told herself. *I just don't want to get into another big hassle with Mom.* Except for asking how the counseling session had gone with Gloria, they hadn't talked about Dad.

Mom talked a lot about Michael, though, and Jennie tried not to listen. And she tried not to notice how happy they were together or how much Nick liked him.

On Thursday Jennie was feeling almost normal again. Mom had invited the whole family to dinner so they could get better acquainted with Michael. As soon as they'd gathered in the living room, Lisa cornered Jennie in the hall. "I've got to tell you something," she whispered. "Let's go to your room."

Once upstairs, Lisa shut the door and leaned against it. "I think you'd better sit down."

"What's going on . . . it's not Gram is it? Has something happened?" Jennie plopped onto the bed. She could tell by Lisa's expression that the news was not going to be good.

"Not Gram," Lisa answered. "Mom said the sheriff had talked with Gram and she's fine. This is about something else. Ah . . . has your mom said anything about Michael lately—I mean about getting married?"

"She said he'd asked her to marry him, but she can't unless Dad is declared legally dead. And that can't happen for two years. Mom's still married to Dad, and if I have anything to say about it, she always will be."

"That's what I was afraid of. Personally, I think you're wrong. I'd think you would want your mom to be happy, and besides, Michael's really nice."

Jennie glared at her.

"But I think I know how you feel," she said quickly. "If anything happened to my dad, I'd probably feel the same way. Anyway, I overheard your mom and mine talking this afternoon. I think your mom and Michael are planning on getting engaged."

"But they can't," Jennie insisted, swallowing back the panic rising inside of her. "It would be wrong. She's still legally married to Dad."

"They can now." Lisa's words hit Jennie with the force of a shotgun blast. "Your mom filed for a divorce."

7

Lisa sat on the bed next to Jennie and draped an arm across her shoulder. "Bummer, huh?"

Jennie didn't answer. What could she say? This was worse than anything she could have imagined. She felt numb, as if all the life had been sucked out of her by some invisible alien.

"I can't believe your mom didn't tell you."

"I think she tried, but I wasn't listening. I was so sure . . ."

"What are you going to do?"

Jennie could only stare at Lisa, as if she were in shock.

————

The announcement came after dinner. A kind of numbness settled over her and lessened the impact when her mom and Michael told the family they were officially engaged.

"I couldn't talk your mother into marrying me, so we compromised and settled on an engagement," Michael had said. "Now all I have to do is get her to set a date." The way he had looked at Mom nearly gagged Jennie. She could imagine how her mom felt. He was so smooth and so nice. No wonder Mom was falling for him. *Oh,*

God, Jennie pleaded. *Make her wait. Remind her how much she loved Dad. I want my dad, God. Not Michael.*

When it was Nick's bedtime, Jennie offered to put him to bed; then after a short story and prayers, she escaped to her room. She doubted Mom would even notice her absence downstairs, and she knew Lisa would understand.

Jennie flopped onto the window seat and leaned back against the pillows. Staring outside into the darkness, she thought again about what she could do. *At least,* Jennie thought, *if I could be with Gram, I wouldn't have to watch. But what if Gram doesn't come home?* She shook her head to cancel the dismal thought. In defiance, Jennie got up and finished packing the rest of her suitcase.

When she'd finished, she snapped the suitcase shut and set it beside her door, then pulled Dad's things from the closet shelf. She put on his old hat and scarf and took the souvenirs out one by one, but it didn't make her feel any better. Jennie picked up his picture and waited for some kind of reassurance. Nothing.

Setting his picture aside, Jennie tried to block out the conflicting voices that filled her head. *Face facts,* one said. *Your father isn't coming back.*

Your mom deserves to be happy, argued another.

You promised your dad you'd hold things together. You messed up.

The voices went on until sleep wiped them away. . . .

In the distance Jennie heard bells. The backyard was full of flowers and ribbon streamers. Mom stood beside Michael wearing a creamy satin gown. Michael put a ring on her finger and bent to kiss her. Jennie felt a presence at her side and looked up. "Dad!"

"How could you let this happen, Princess?" He

frowned. His sad, blue eyes ripped at her heart.

"I'm sorry, Daddy." Jennie tried to put her arms around him and felt only air.

"So am I, Princess. So am I."

Jennie grabbed for his hand. "Wait!" she cried to the fading image. "Daddy, don't leave me. I need you."

"I can't stay. There's no place for me here. You have Michael now."

"No! Daddy, please, don't go . . . please . . ." The bells rang harder and louder. Finally she awoke enough to recognize the sound and reached for the phone.

"Hello?" Jennie mumbled into the mouthpiece.

"Were you sleeping? It's only nine, I thought you'd still be up."

"Ryan." Jennie unfolded her cramped legs and groaned. "I must have fallen asleep." She rubbed her eyes. The news about Mom filing for divorce and announcing her engagement spilled out of her. Then she told him about the dream. She was glad when he didn't remind her of how childish she sounded.

"Hey, listen," Ryan said in a soothing tone. "Your dad would never blame you for what your mom's doing."

"I should have stopped her." Jennie cleared her dad's stuff off the bed and flopped back onto it.

"It's not your fault. I don't know if it will help, but I was really shook when Mom divorced my dad. I was only eight, but I figured the whole thing was my fault. Like if I'd been a better kid it wouldn't have happened. Kids do that kind of thing. Blame themselves. At least that's what Mom told me."

Jennie let out a sigh that came from somewhere around her toes. "Thanks. I know you're right, but I still feel like I ruined everything. Besides, the dream was right, in a way. If Mom marries Michael and Dad comes back, he won't be able to stay."

"Not with you, but you'll be able to see him."

"I suppose."

"Hey . . . listen, I called to tell you about the house."

"Is Gram home?"

"No, but I thought I'd better let you know what happened."

There was a long pause, and Jennie prodded, "So, are you going to tell me or what?"

"You've already been through a lot today . . ."

"Ryan, don't do this to me. Talk."

"Okay, okay. Anyway, I went over to get her mail and put it on her kitchen counter like I usually do. When I walked in I heard something in the living room and then heard the front door close."

"Did you see who it was?"

"It was getting dark, but I saw this big guy running down the road. He drove off in a dark-colored car, maybe navy blue or black. I couldn't see what make, and it was too far away to read the license. I went after him, but by the time I got to the road he was gone."

"Did you call the sheriff?"

"Yeah. They dusted the place for prints, but the guy must have been wearing gloves."

"Did he steal anything?"

"No. They figured I surprised him, and he took off before he could take anything. They're going to beef up their patrol of the neighborhood." He hesitated, then added, "I noticed something odd, though. Someone had switched off the answering machine."

"You mean the burglar was listening to her messages?"

"Looks that way. I checked around and nothing else seems to have been disturbed."

"Weird. It doesn't make sense. He must have been after something else. That settles it. I've got to get down there. I need to search the house. I'll be able to tell if anything's missing. And if the guy comes back, I could . . ."

"What? Get yourself killed? No way, Jennie. Not a good idea. Besides, your mom will never let you stay down here alone. And even if she did, what would you do about school? I know it's hard to do, but we really ought to let Sheriff Taylor handle things."

"I suppose you're right." An idea had begun to form, but Jennie couldn't tell Ryan about it, not yet anyway. She thanked him for calling, and he mumbled something about having sweet dreams. Unfortunately, the way things were going Jennie had a feeling they'd be about as sweet as lemon juice.

The next morning Jennie told Mom she'd go to the counseling camp the first week of June, but only if Lisa could go along. Both Mom and Gloria agreed.

"This will be good for you," Mom said. "I'm glad you've decided to go."

Jennie felt like a scuz ball for what she was about to do. "Yeah, I'm sure everything will work out okay, Mom," Jennie stated. That, at least, was the truth.

———

"No way," Lisa muttered, digging into her bowl of chocolate-covered nuts and rich ice cream. "I don't care if it'll get me to the beach for a week. I won't do it."

"Lisa, you owe me. Think about all the times I've helped you with your homework." Jennie had planned her escape to Gram's house perfectly but had to convince Lisa to play her part.

"This has got to be the dumbest scheme you've ever come up with." Lisa stretched across Jennie's bed on her stomach and shook her head.

Jennie wove her braid through her fingers and walked back and forth across the area rug in front of Lisa. "It will work. By the time Mom figures out what happened, I'll have found Gram." *I hope.* "Anyway, I've got to go. She could be in real trouble." Jennie told Lisa about the answering machine and the mysterious stranger Ryan had seen leaving Gram's house.

Lisa frowned and waved her spoon in the air. "Maybe you should talk to the police."

"Ryan has been talking to Sheriff Taylor, but they haven't come up with anything."

"I think you're making a big thing out of this. Gram called the Johnsons. She was fine."

"What if someone made her call?" Jennie knelt in front of Lisa and looked her in the eye. "What if she's being held prisoner and whoever is holding her wants us to believe she's safe? Doesn't it seem strange to you that Gram would call the Johnsons and the sheriff, but not us?"

"Maybe she tried to and we weren't home."

"We both have answering machines." Jennie retrieved the note Gram had sent from her jeans pocket and handed it to Lisa. "Here, read this."

Lisa read it and handed it back. "Where did this come from?"

"Gram mailed it the day she was due back from Canada. It's postmarked *Lincoln City*. Something really strange is going on, and I need to get down there. Gram is trying to tell me something in this note, but I haven't been able to figure out what."

"I don't know. I think you should show this to our parents."

"Yeah, right. They'd just say Gram is getting old and forgetful. I even thought that at first. You've got to help me, Lisa. What if something really has happened to Gram? I need to get to her house. There might be some clues the sheriff has overlooked."

Lisa sat up and folded her legs Indian-style. The frown on her forehead told Jennie her cousin was relenting. "Lisa," she pleaded. "We've got to try. My plan will work—I know it will."

"This is insane. How can I take your place at camp when we're both registered?"

"Easy. We'll call and cancel yours. When we get there, I'll leave and you'll be me."

"What if I get caught? What about your counselor—she'll know I'm a phoney."

"Gloria won't be there. No one there will have seen me. All you have to do is pretend you're Jennie McGrady, the troubled teenager who's still grieving over her missing father. One week. Please Lisa. I'd do it for you."

Lisa drew in a deep breath and blew it out her mouth.

"There's another reason I have to go." Tears stung Jennie's eyes. "I'm supposed to spend the summer with Gram. I can't take the chance on Mom changing her mind. I have to get out of here, Lisa. This thing with Mom and Michael is tearing me apart. I may not be able to stop them, but if I'm with Gram . . ." Jennie stopped to blow her nose. She didn't dare tell Lisa the other reason—not yet. Maybe later, after she had a chance to talk to Gram.

"Okay. I'll do it. But I still think it's nuts. If our parents find out they'll kill us both."

"*If* they find out we'll be worse than dead. But they can't find out. Not if we don't tell anyone—so don't— not even Brad."

"What are you going to do about Ryan? If you show up down there alone, he's going to wonder what's going on."

"He won't. Trust me. This is the most foolproof plan I've ever come up with."

"That's what you said about our little trip to Disneyland. Remember? 'They won't find out,' you said."

Jennie cringed. "Well, they wouldn't have if that highway patrolman hadn't been cruising by when we walked out of the woods. Besides, we were only ten. And how was I to know the camp director checked all the kids in? We should have gone to camp first, then escaped."

"We shouldn't have tried to go at all." Lisa licked the last of her ice cream off the spoon. "Do you realize how dangerous that was? It's a good thing that patrolman picked us up."

"You're right. It was a dumb move, but this is different. Gram may be in danger."

"I shouldn't do this."

"But you will," Jennie said as she sat beside Lisa on the bed. They were taking a big chance, but the more Jennie thought about it, the more convinced she became. She had to find Gram even if it meant risking everything to do it.

Camp was scheduled to start on Monday at a retreat center on the southern Washington coast. Jennie planned to drive the two of them up on Sunday, drop Lisa off, and head south, across the Columbia River to Astoria, then down the Oregon coast to Gram's. She'd find out what was going on with Gram, and at the end of the week, pick Lisa up and head home.

Lisa stayed over on Saturday night so they could get an early start. Mom had fussed over them all morning, and they were just getting ready to pull out of the driveway when Michael drove in behind them, blocking their way. "Now what?" Jennie groaned under her breath.

"I'm glad I caught you. Hang on. I've got a great idea, but I need to talk to your mom."

He bounded up the steps and walked into the house without ringing the bell. "I can't believe it." Jennie stared after him. "Did you see that? He acts like he lives here."

"He practically does," Lisa said. When Jennie glared at her, she insisted, "Well, he does. And he will be when they get married."

"Whose side are you on, anyway?"

Before Lisa could answer, Mom opened the car door on Lisa's side. "Michael has offered to drive us all down to the beach. Isn't that great! We can do some exploring at Fort Canby before we take you girls to camp."

Panic rose in Jennie's stomach like a tidal wave. "B-b-but, Mom . . . how are we going to get back home?"

"We'll come get you. The coast is wonderful this time of year, and I've been wanting to visit the Peninsula for ages."

"But there's no room . . ."

"Don't be silly. We'll take the Buick," Mom countered.

"We're late . . . there's no time."

"Nick and I are dressed. By the time you girls get yourselves situated in the backseat of the Buick, we'll be ready to go. I'll get our jackets."

"What was it you said about having all the angles covered?" Lisa asked in her I-told-you-so voice as soon as the car door shut.

"I'll think of something," Jennie said with a lot more confidence than she felt.

8

For the first half hour of their trip, Jennie read books to Nick and tried to block out the fact that Mom and Michael were in the front seat talking like Dad and Mom used to. *Well, not exactly,* Jennie thought, grimacing. When her dad was home, there were a lot of arguments between her parents. An awful lot.

A scene from the past slid unbidden into Jennie's mind and began to play out like a movie. . . . *Jennie sat between her parents and leaned against her father, pretending to be asleep.*

"The chief called last night," Dad said.

Mom sighed. "Oh no, not again. Jason, you just got home. When do you have to go?"

"Tonight."

"Tonight? But what about Jennie's birthday? You promised her you'd take her to the amusement park."

"I'll take her when I get back. She won't mind. She understands about my work."

"For how long, Jason?" Mom asked in an accusing tone. "How long will she put up with you putting your job ahead of your family?" She rushed on, "And what about me?"

Dad's fist slammed into the steering wheel and startled Jennie. "Why do you always have to fight me on this?" he

71

hissed. "*You knew what it would be like before you married me.*"

"*Daddy?*" Jennie looked up into her father's angry face and began to cry. Through a screen of tears she watched his features soften. "*I'm sorry we woke you, Princess,*" he said, smiling down at her. "*Your mother and I were just talking. It's okay. Go back to sleep.*"

Jennie shook the memory out of her thoughts. That day, her father had left after dinner and had never come home. Jennie felt a wetness on her cheeks and whisked it away. She didn't want to think about the bad times. She only wanted to remember the good ones, the fun they'd had together. Besides, maybe if Mom had been more understanding they wouldn't have argued. She pushed the memory away, and a few minutes later sleep wiped away her thoughts.

Jennie didn't stir until Michael turned off the motor. "C'mon, you sleepyheads. I've got just the thing to wake you up."

Jennie rubbed her eyes. "Where are we?"

"At the U.S. Coast Guard Station near Ilwaco. We go through here to get to the lighthouse at the top of the hill. C'mon, Susan, let's race these kids up the hill."

Jennie looked up the hill and back at Mom. Michael was crazy if he thought Mom was going to race up that. Jennie's mouth dropped open when her mom took Michael's outstretched hand and started running. "See you kids at the top!" she called over her shoulder, laughing.

"Hey!" Lisa grabbed Jennie's arm and pulled her along. "This looks like a neat place. The scenery's great."

One look around and Jennie could tell Lisa wasn't talking about the view. Four guys in uniform walked out of one of the buildings and came toward them.

"Aren't they cute?" Lisa asked.

"I'm shocked," Jennie teased. "I thought you and Brad were going steady."

"We are, but that doesn't mean I can't look. Besides, maybe we can find one for you."

Jennie rolled her eyes. "Come on." She grabbed Nick's hand and started for the hill, wanting to get Lisa away from the guys before she embarrassed them both.

Lisa, Nick, and Jennie took off up the trail, passing the adults. While they waited for Mom and Michael to huff and puff their way up, they pressed against the cyclone fence and watched the surf crash against the craggy outcropping of rocks below.

"Look at all the boats!" Nick pointed to a dozen or so spots bobbing in the distance.

For the next two hours they hiked trails and explored the coastline. Nick jabbered on about the boats, the fishes, and the ocean. Mom and Michael must have taken a hundred pictures before Mom announced that it was time to go.

Jennie's heart thundered inside her chest as they climbed into the car. *Calm down, McGrady,* she told herself. *There's an answer. Just don't panic.* When they stopped at a country store in Ocean Park, she found a solution. The bus. It would take longer and cost more, but she could still get to Gram's.

Jennie almost suffered another setback when they arrived at the camp and Mom insisted on coming in to help them register and find their rooms. "Mom," Jennie said, "we're sixteen years old and perfectly capable of checking in by ourselves."

Jennie thought for a minute she'd object, but Michael interrupted. "Jennie's got a point. I remember how embarrassing it was for me when I was that age to have my mother hovering over me."

He winked and Jennie threw him a grateful smile. Michael could be a really nice guy. She decided that if Mom had to marry someone, Michael was a good choice. *But she has no business getting married,* a voice inside her reminded. A feeling of sympathy washed over Jennie. None of this was really Michael's fault. All he'd really done was get mixed up with the wrong family at the wrong time.

After Mom and Nick hugged Lisa and Jennie a dozen times, the three of them piled into the car and drove off. Lisa and Jennie stood beside their bags and waved good-bye until the Buick was out of sight.

"Whew," Jennie sighed after they'd gone. "That was close."

"This is not going well. Maybe we'd both better check in. I'm not cut out for all this sneaking around."

"The worst is over. In case Mom and Michael are still around, I'll walk out by way of the beach. It's only a couple of miles to town and I can catch the bus there." Jennie examined the bus schedule she'd picked up at the store earlier.

"Do you have enough money?"

"I think so. I took fifty dollars out of my savings account on Friday."

Lisa dug around in her oversized bag. "Here." She handed Jennie a twenty. "Just in case you run short. Call me when you get in."

"Thanks. I'm not sure I can get through to you. Maybe you'd better phone me at Gram's. I should be there by nine tonight."

"That's six hours!"

"I know. Wish me luck."

"Yeah," she whispered into Jennie's hair as they hugged each other. "I'll pray. You'll need a lot more than wishes."

Jennie hoisted her bag over her shoulder and headed toward the beach.

———

"I will never ride another bus as long as I live," she muttered as she slipped a key into Gram's door. She'd had to wait hours between stops, and when she finally caught the bus to Bay Village, it stopped at least a hundred times along the way. Jennie didn't get into town until nine-thirty. She was about to call Ryan to pick her up when Gram's other neighbors, the Pecks, offered her a ride.

Jennie pushed the door open, stepped inside, and switched on the entry light. That's when she smelled it. A man's aftershave. Jennie thought about the man Ryan had seen running from the house. She wasn't up to facing a burglar on her own.

Jennie took a deep breath and concentrated on getting out of the house as quietly as possible. Once outside, she dragged in another gulp of air and looked around. High rhododendron bushes and trees cast spooky-looking shadows over the lawn. *Shadows or not, McGrady, you can't stand here all night*. She took off running for the weeping willow tree, which stood between the two lots. The long sweeping limbs hung to the ground, providing the perfect hiding place. Pressing herself against its ancient bark, she inched her way to the other side where she'd have a straight shot at Ryan's house.

Her hand touched something fleshy. She tried to scream, but the sound caught in her throat and came out sounding like a *meow* from a sick cat. Jennie yanked back her hand and dove through the screen of willow branches.

She went down. The attacker sprawled on top of her. Jennie couldn't move. Or breathe.

"One false move and you're dead." The voice was raspy, but recognizable.

"Ryan?"

"Jennie!" he gasped. "What the heck are you doing here?" He rolled off her and groaned. "You scared me half to death."

Jennie was hauling in air, still waiting for her heart to stop pounding when Ryan jumped to his feet. He reached down to give her a hand up and pulled her so hard she crashed into him. "Hey, take it easy. What's with you, anyway? I thought you'd be glad to see me."

Ryan brushed off his clothes, then stood staring at her. At least she thought he was staring. It was a little too dark to tell. "I am. I mean, I'm glad it was you and not that guy I saw the other night. I just didn't expect you to be prowling around in the middle of the night. You could have been hurt. Does your mom know you're here?"

It wasn't exactly the middle of the night, but Jennie didn't bother to correct him. She also ignored his remark about her mom. Jennie huffed. "You think I expected you? What are you doing lurking around out here, anyway?"

"I came over because I heard a car and saw the entry light on. I thought maybe that guy I'd seen the other night was back." Ryan sighed and started toward Gram's house. "Let's go inside," he muttered. "It's cold out here."

"Wait! I think someone's in there." Jennie explained about coming in and smelling a man's cologne. "I was coming over to get you."

He looked at her for a second, then said, "Wait here. I'll check the house."

"I'm going with you."

"Jennie, if he's still in there . . ."

"We'll be stronger as a team." She grabbed his arm and pulled him forward.

"Well, at least let me go ahead of you." On that point, Jennie didn't argue. They may have been close in height, but he was definitely stronger. She rubbed her backside. By tomorrow she'd have the bruises to prove it.

They searched the house, but whoever had been there was gone. Their search ended in the kitchen. "I don't like it." Ryan checked the lock on the back door. "You shouldn't be staying here alone."

"I'll be fine." She said it more to convince herself than Ryan. Even though they hadn't found anyone in the house, Jennie didn't want Ryan to leave. "Want some hot chocolate or something?" she asked.

"Sure." Ryan pulled a chair from the table, spun it around and sat down. Propping his arms on the chair back, he rested his chin on his hands. "Ah . . . I'm sorry I flattened you out there. I mean . . . you could have been hurt."

"It's okay." Jennie filled two cups with water and stuck them in the microwave. "I should have called you. Actually, I was going to have you pick me up, but the Pecks offered me a ride."

"Hmmm." Ryan stretched and yawned. "If I wasn't so tired I'd be mad at you. Why'd you come down here at this time of night, anyway?"

Jennie winced. "I hadn't planned on that." She told Ryan about her plan to drive down and how Mom and Michael messed things up.

"Serves you right," he said in a tone that sounded a little too parental. "I think you better call your mom in the morning and have her come get you."

"Forget it." Jennie set the hot chocolate on the table. Ryan turned around to face the table as Jennie slipped into the chair next to him. "I've gone through a lot to get down here so I could find out what's happened to Gram. I *know* she's in some sort of trouble. I'd like your help, but if you're going to come off acting like my mother, I'll do this alone."

Ryan took a sip of his chocolate and licked the foamy mustache from his lip. He wasn't agreeing, but he wasn't saying no, either. "Look," Jennie continued, "I'll admit coming down here in the dark wasn't the smartest thing I've ever done, but I was desperate. Being with Gram this summer is really important to me. Besides, you know how I feel about her. If something's happened . . . I have to find her, Ryan, I just have to."

Ryan frowned. "I thought we decided she was working undercover and that we'd better stay out of it."

"I know. It's just . . . I mean it doesn't make sense. Even if she were working on a case she'd call her family. And why call you from Canada, when she mailed a note to me from the coast the day before? She's trying to tell me something. I just wish I knew what."

"Did you bring the note with you?"

"It's in my pack."

"Can I see it? Maybe if we look at it together and talk about it, we can come up with something."

"Sure, I'll get . . ."

Wham! The door slammed open. Jennie screamed. Ryan sprang to his feet. His chair crashed to the floor.

"Police! Freeze!" Two men appeared in the open doorway holding guns.

"Up against the wall! Now! Move!"

The first thing Jennie thought about was that now she knew what TV detectives meant about "looking down the business end of a gun." Her second thought was that she wouldn't make it to Florida or anywhere else—ever. And third, she was glad Mom and Nick had Michael because they'd have someone to take care of them when the cops came to tell her Jennie was dead.

All these thoughts came in a matter of a second or two. When the guns didn't go off, Jennie chanced a look over her shoulder at the men holding them.

One was a gorgeous young guy who looked like he could have been a male model. Unfortunately, this wasn't a studio and no one was taking pictures. Jennie shifted her gaze to the silver-haired man beside him.

She'd known Sheriff Taylor for years. He dropped over to see Gram a couple times a week to have one of Gram's great pies. She'd never been afraid of him—until now. But then he'd never pointed a gun at her before, either.

Sheriff Taylor held a gun on them while the cute one frisked them up and down. Jennie opened her mouth to object, but nothing came out.

"What's going on, Sheriff?" Ryan asked.

"I'll ask the questions here," he growled. "Joe!" The sheriff signaled the dark-haired man, who Jennie guessed was his deputy. "Watch these two while I check the house."

"Y-you can't do that . . . can they, Ryan?" Jennie asked, trying to dislodge the lump of panic that blocked her throat. "Don't they need some kind of search warrant or something?"

"I think they have one . . ."

"Quiet." The sheriff waved his gun in the direction of the table. "Sit over here. Hands on the table where I can see them." The sheriff moved around to the opposite side of the table and leaned toward Jennie and Ryan. His face had the wrinkled look of a bulldog, only he was chewing a toothpick instead of a bone. If he was trying to intimidate them, it worked . . . on Jennie at least.

He straightened and waited until Joe had them in his sights, then left the room.

No one spoke. Joe was holding the gun with both hands, and Jennie was sure he'd shoot them if they so much as scratched their noses. So, they sat there, hands spread flat out on the table as they'd been told. The clock on the stove ticked. Ten-thirty. Jennie could hear the heavy footfall of the sheriff overhead. He was in Gram's room, pushing the hangers back and forth along the rod in her closet. Tick-tock. Tick-tock. Ten thirty-five. The bathroom, lifting the lid on the toilet tank. Tick-tock. Tick-tock. Ten thirty-eight.

"Nothing," the sheriff said as he reappeared in the kitchen. "If she was here, she's gone now."

Sheriff Taylor looked hard at Jennie, then at Ryan. "All right, where is she?"

"Who?" Ryan asked.

"Don't play games with me *Mr.* Johnson. If you know where she is you'll tell me or we'll book you and your girlfriend here as accomplices."

"If you're talking about Gram, we don't know where she is," Jennie said.

"Well then, suppose you tell us who you are and what you're doing in Helen McGrady's house."

Jennie was surprised he hadn't recognized her. Well, maybe that wasn't so strange. She had grown at least a foot since he'd last seen her, and hopefully she'd developed in a few places as well. "I . . . I'm Jennie . . . her granddaughter," she stammered. "I'm staying here for a few days."

The sheriff straightened and grinned. "Jennie. I didn't recognize you. You're all grown up. Turned into a mighty pretty young lady."

Her neck was getting stiff, or maybe she was just embarrassed. She reached up to massage the knot in her muscles.

"Hold it!" Joe commanded and pointed the gun at her again.

"Why are you doing this?" Jennie half yelled and half cried. "Can't you just leave us alone? We haven't done anything wrong." It was probably the wrong thing to say to two armed men, but at that point Jennie was so frustrated she didn't really care. "I came down here to find my grandmother, and all of a sudden I'm caught in the middle of some weird scene that makes the Twilight Zone look normal. I don't care if you *are* the sheriff! You don't have any right to come in here and treat us like criminals. You should be helping us find Gram, not harassing us." Jennie took a ragged breath. "Gram is your friend. Why are you acting like this?"

There was a long pause, then Joe cleared his throat and said, "We through here, Sam?"

Sheriff Taylor nodded, then rubbed a tanned, age-spotted hand across his silvered beard. "I'm sorry if we were a little rough with you. But we're investigating a serious crime here. Can't be too careful." He turned to his deputy. "Better take a look outside before we head back to the station." Joe holstered his gun as they headed for the door.

"Wait a minute," Jennie called to their retreating figures. "Aren't you going to tell us what this is all about?"

The sheriff sauntered back and leaned across the table, a frown deepening the lines on his forehead. His pale, blue eyes had kind of a misty look. "Helen McGrady isn't missing, Jennie. She's a fugitive. We have a warrant for her arrest."

9

Jennie gasped and sank into the chair she'd just vacated. "That's impossible. Gram would never break the law."

"A couple of weeks ago," Joe said, "a gang heisted over a million dollars worth of diamonds from a trade show in Portland. We have reason to believe your grandmother was involved."

"Yes. So naturally, Jennie, if your grandmother contacts you, or if you think you know of her whereabouts, we expect to be told, *immediately*." Sheriff Taylor smiled, but his eyes had grown cold.

After they'd gone, Jennie sat in the chair and stared at the sea gulls on her cup. How ironic. She remembered hearing about the robbery and wanting to tell Gram. And now the sheriff thought Gram had done it. Jennie wasn't sure how long she and Ryan sat there. After a while he removed the cup from her grip and took hold of her hand.

Jennie looked up at him. "She didn't do it."

"I know," he said. "But if you're going to sit here all night, we'll never find out who did, or how Gram got mixed up in it."

"Oh, Ryan. Thank you." Jennie threw herself into his arms. She wasn't sure who was more surprised. She'd never before thrown herself at a boy. But he hugged her back . . . at least she thought it was a hug. Jennie had acted on impulse and suddenly felt stupid. "Sorry," she murmured as she backed away.

"No problem." Ryan grinned and stuffed his hands in his pockets.

"You'll really help me find Gram?" Jennie asked. He nodded. Then remembering what he'd said earlier, she added, "And you won't call my mom?"

He shrugged. "I'll leave that to you."

Relieved, Jennie took the pad and pen out of her bag and showed Ryan the notes she'd made about the case during the long bus ride. As Ryan watched, Jennie wrote in the last incident about the sheriff wanting to arrest Gram for stealing diamonds.

"This is impossible," she moaned. "It's like putting together a puzzle with most of the pieces missing."

"Maybe we need some more puzzle pieces." Ryan leaned back in the chair, balancing on its back legs. "And some fresh air." He let the chair bounce back and jumped up. "Let's go down to the beach. Maybe we can concentrate better there."

"Sounds perfect." They grabbed their jackets, hit the door running, and didn't slow down until they reached the rocky path that led to the surf about a quarter of a mile from Gram's house. The sand had been swallowed up by a high tide, so they sat on the cliff and watched the churning white water below.

Saltwater slivers sprayed her face as waves thundered against the rocks. Big, threatening, and dangerous as the ocean was, it always made Jennie feel safe, as though a bigger Presence existed out there, who set it all in motion and who looked after her.

"Do you believe in God?" Jennie asked suddenly. The moon broke through the clouds, lighting up the darkness.

A lopsided smile crossed Ryan's face. "Most of the time. Why do you ask?"

She shrugged her shoulders. "I don't know. When I'm out here looking at all this, I think there must be a God. And when everything is going good, I guess I don't think too much about it. But when Dad disappeared, and now, with Gram missing and Mom getting engaged . . . I just wonder. I mean if there's a God in control of everything, why do bad things happen? Why does everything get so messed up?"

"Hey," Ryan said as he settled an arm across Jennie's shoulders, "maybe we ought to solve the mystery of your missing grandmother before we work on the mysteries of the universe."

Jennie smiled and looked up at him. "Got any ideas?" She didn't know about Ryan, but all of a sudden Jennie had a head full of ideas, and they had nothing whatsoever to do with Gram or God. Ryan's face was only about three inches from hers, and she could hardly breathe. She'd had butterflies knocking around in her stomach before, but now it felt like the whole flock had taken off at once. He was going to kiss her.

Yes. Jennie closed her eyes. *No.* She opened them again. Kissing Ryan would change everything between them. She wasn't ready for that. Maybe Ryan felt the same way, maybe he sensed her withdrawal. At any rate he squeezed her shoulder and stood. "It's getting late. Maybe we'd better get some sleep and work on finding Gram in the morning."

"Yeah." Jennie felt relieved and disappointed all at the same time.

They didn't talk on the way back to the house. Things had definitely changed. She used to be so comfortable with him. Now Jennie felt awkward, like she'd gone into a stranger's house and didn't know quite how to act or what to expect.

When they got to Gram's, Ryan leaned against the door, trapping her head between his hands. "I still don't feel comfortable about your staying here alone. Especially not with that guy roaming around. Why don't you get your things and bunk at my place? You can have the guest room. Mom and Dad won't mind."

"No, I'll be fine. I'll lock and bolt the doors. And there's a phone by Gram's bed. I can call you if I hear anything."

Ryan didn't argue. He seemed relieved. Maybe he needed his space as much as Jennie needed hers. Before he left, he kissed her. Just sort of brushed his lips against hers. The kiss was soft and feathery, but it skittered through her like an electric shock.

"Ah . . . I'll be over at seven. We can talk before I go to school."

Jennie nodded, backed into the house, and bolted the door. She hung up her coat, wandered into the living room, locked the front door, and sank into Gram's rocking chair.

Things were getting too complicated and out of control. Jennie preferred simple. She wanted her mom back to being Mom, not some starry-eyed romantic swooning over her new love. She wanted her dad. She wanted Gram and their trip to Florida. And Ryan? She wasn't sure what she wanted with Ryan.

All this was scrambling around in her head when Jennie noticed the flashing red light on Gram's answering machine. She rewound the tape, then sat back to listen.

"Hi, Mum. It's Kate. What are you up to this time? I'm getting worried. Call me."

"Helen." A man's voice—a deep one, with an English accent. "We've done it, Luv. Time to come home."

Jennie replayed it. "James Bond," she said aloud. No kidding, the guy sounded like Sean Connery. What had they done? He'd called her love? Was he a friend?

Since Jennie was too wired to sleep, she decided to have a look around. Gram's desk was a disaster, as usual. Leafing through the piles of papers stacked all over the desk, she found copies of articles she'd sent out, tear sheets, a dozen or so Post-it notes, and some newspaper and magazine clippings. Jennie could almost hear Gram saying, "A neat desk is a sign of a sick mind." If that was true Gram had to have the healthiest mind in the country. She wondered if the man Ryan had seen running from the house a few days ago had been through Gram's papers. Probably. She rubbed her arms to chase away the chill.

Unable to find anything in Grams's files, Jennie switched on the computer and accessed Gram's directories. She'd nearly finished reading the list when she saw it. "JB." This was too much of a coincidence. Could this file have something to do with the mysterious voice on the phone? Gram and Jennie often had the same impressions. Did Gram think he sounded like James Bond too? When she moved the cursor down to the JB directory and tried to access it, the screen went blank. Almost immediately a message appeared at the bottom of the screen. *Enter Code Name:*

Strange. Gram didn't usually bother with codes. Jennie tried another directory, one named "Sunset," and got right in. She then accessed a file labeled "Frisco" and found an article Gram had written on the sights and sounds of San Francisco, for Travel Magazine. She tried a couple more and gained immediate access. Then she went back to JB. When it asked for a code name she typed in "Bond."

ACCESS DENIED! The screen flashed its warning then asked for a code name again. For about half an hour Jennie typed in names and numbers she thought Gram might use. Nothing.

Weary, she rubbed her burning eyes and massaged her neck, then switched off the computer and headed upstairs. It was after midnight by the time she'd brushed her teeth and slipped into her nightgown. Jennie crawled under the covers and turned out the light. The sheets felt cool and smelled fresh. The ocean sounds from beyond the open window lulled her to sleep.

Ryan's six-forty-five phone call awakened her. "You have fifteen minutes to make yourself beautiful and fix me some breakfast," he said.

"In your dreams, Johnson," Jennie mumbled and hung up. If he wanted beautiful he'd have a long wait. Breakfast she could handle. Jennie thought about what Sheriff Taylor had said, then squashed the thought. *You are not pretty, McGrady. You're too thin, too tall, and . . .* Jennie tossed that thought aside as well.

In the bathroom Jennie took a long objective look at herself—something she hadn't done since she was about thirteen. Actually, she didn't look half bad. She did have great hair. And her eyes were okay. In fact, Lisa had told her she had eyes to die for, which, simply translated, meant thick, long lashes that didn't need mascara.

Okay, so maybe she was pretty—in a plain sort of way. At any rate, Jennie hoped Ryan would think so. She managed to comb her hair, drag on jeans and a sweater, and was halfway finished making the eggs by the time Ryan knocked on the back door.

"Hey, I was only kidding." Ryan hung his jacket on the coat rack by the kitchen door and sprawled onto a chair. "I didn't really expect you to cook me breakfast."

"Don't tell me you've already eaten."

"No, but . . ."

"Good, then sit down and eat." Jennie slid a plate of scrambled eggs, bacon, and toast onto the table in front of him. "I don't mind, really. It's the least I can do since you've agreed to help me find Gram."

"Where did you find the food? Gram usually leaves the fridge and cupboards bare when she's gone."

Jennie felt as if she'd been hit in the stomach. Ryan was right. Gram never left food in her fridge when she went on trips. "It was all in here last night. You don't suppose it could have been the burglar, do you?"

"That's nuts." Ryan got up and poked around in the cupboards. "Why would a burglar stock the kitchen, unless . . ."

"He . . . he's planning to stay?" Jennie jumped up and grabbed Ryan's arm. "He could be here right now," she squeaked.

"I don't think so. I have a feeling Gram did this. This is the kind of stuff she buys." He pried Jennie's hand off his arm and dragged her to the fridge. "Look, 1% milk, yogurt, and this bread . . ." He lifted the loaf from the counter. "Whole grain. This is the stuff she uses."

"So Gram was here." Jennie sank into a chair by the table. "I knew it."

Ryan shook his head. "She must have come in during the day when we were all out."

"Which means she did come home from Canada like she'd planned." Jennie slapped her palm against her forehead. "What an airhead I've been! I can't believe I didn't think of it before. The airline will have a record of her flight. All we have to do is call and see if she came back that day."

Jennie left Ryan to eat while she called Alaska Airlines.

"Bingo," she said as she hung up the phone and walked back to the kitchen. "Gram arrived in Portland on the twenty-third. She probably stopped by the store for groceries on the way down."

"And at the post office in Lincoln City, where she mailed the note to you."

"But what happened after that?"

The tea kettle whistled. Jennie fixed some of Gram's peppermint tea and sat down at the table. She told Ryan about the inaccessible directory in Gram's computer and the man who had called.

"Whew," he whistled. "I don't get it. It seems like the deeper we go into this thing, the more confusing it gets."

"It feels like one of those stupid math problems . . . if the square root of a is b, what is the square root of d?"

Ryan laughed. "So let's use a little logic. If none of these pieces fit, we must be missing something major, right?"

Ryan stretched out, tipped his chair back on two legs, and stared at the ceiling.

After a few minutes his chair settled back on all fours. "The note. We were going to look at it last night before the sheriff blew in. I don't know if it would help, but I'd like to see it."

"Sure." Jennie ran upstairs, pulled the note out of her pack, and hurried back to the kitchen. She listened as he read it aloud.

"*I'm sorry I haven't been able to call.*" Ryan paused and glanced up at her. "Does that mean she wanted to?"

"Or . . . maybe it means she *couldn't* call. Like, someone was holding her prisoner and wouldn't let her."

"Okay, let's say that's the case. That means the rest of her note is a code as well. *If anything happens to me . . .*"

"She's worried that she might be hurt . . . or killed." Jennie closed her eyes and held her stomach. "I'm not sure I can do this."

"We have to, Jennie. If something really has happened to her, we've got to figure out what she means." Ryan read the last phrase. "*I want you to have the bracelet we found last summer.* Okay, now tell me about this bracelet."

"It's an antique. Costume jewelry—rhinestones. When we first found it we thought they might be diamonds."

"Where did you find it?"

"That's it! I've been so busy concentrating on the bracelet, I didn't even think about where we found it." Jennie charged up the stairs and into Gram's closet, Ryan following close behind. "Turn on the light, will you?"

Ryan pulled the cord that hung from the closet ceiling. "What are you doing?"

"This is where we found the bracelet." Jennie knelt down and felt along the back wall until she found a ridge. Lifting out a square panel, she shoved her hand through an opening. Her fingers brushed against something. "Feels like paper. This wasn't in here last summer," Jennie said, lifting out a large brown grocery bag.

"You want to open it or should I?" Ryan asked.

"You do it." Jennie held her breath as Ryan unrolled the top of the sack and looked in. "Ah . . . I don't think you want to see this, Jennie."

She didn't. Unfortunately, Jennie couldn't keep from looking. Inside the bag, nestled among layers of white tissue and newspaper, lay dozens of diamond pendants, necklaces, and bracelets.

10

Ryan lifted a necklace from the bag. "This thing has to be worth a fortune. There must be fifty diamonds in this one alone."

Jennie watched it slither out of his hand, moving and shimmering as if it were alive. It caught the morning light and glistened like fire on ice.

She grabbed the necklace and stuffed it back in the sack.

"What are you doing?"

"I don't know how Gram got this stuff, but if the sheriff finds out . . ." Jennie's heart was pounding so hard she could hardly think. She tucked the bag back in its hiding place, slipped the panel back in place, and closed the closet door. "We need to keep this hidden. It proves Gram had something to do with the robbery."

"You think Gram is a thief?"

"N . . . no," Jennie stammered, "of course not. It's just . . . Oh, Ryan, I don't know what to think."

Ryan hooked his arm around her neck. "I know this doesn't look good, but we need to stay calm. There's a perfectly good explanation."

Jennie didn't know why she found his comment so funny, but she started laughing. "Right," she hooted. "I can just hear it all now. 'Gram, why are there stolen diamonds in your closet?' And she'd smile at me and say, 'It's quite simple really, my dear. I'm an international jewel thief.'

" 'Oh, how interesting,' I'd say. 'Have you been in the business long?' " Jennie hiccupped. "This isn't funny, Ryan . . . why am I laughing?"

"You're hysterical."

"Hic . . . that's ridiculous. I never get hysterical." He was right, except for one thing. Jennie had gone a step beyond hysterical. She was a nut case. She hiccupped again.

"Come on." Ryan grabbed Jennie's hand and pulled her down the stairs and into the kitchen. He handed her a small paper bag. "Breathe into this."

Jennie slid down into a chair, and after a few deep breaths, felt the panic edge away. Ryan reheated the tea she'd fixed for breakfast, then knelt beside her and wrapped her hands around the warm cup.

"Drink it."

She did. After a few sips sanity had returned and with it the cold reality of the secret panel, the diamonds hidden there, and the very real possibility that her own grandmother had stolen them. "What am I going to do?"

"We," he corrected. "What are *we* going to do."

Jennie smiled. "Okay, partner, got any ideas?"

"Just one. We both know Gram isn't a thief. For one thing, she doesn't need the money. And if she had stolen them, she'd never implicate you. So we start from that premise."

"She wrote to me because I'm the only one who knows about the hiding place. She got them somehow . . . maybe from the real thieves. Maybe she found out who did it and . . ."

Ryan shook his head. "No, that doesn't make sense. If she knew who stole the diamonds in the first place, she'd go to the police and have them arrested. She sure wouldn't keep them herself."

"Then why are they here?"

"Who knows? Like you said before, there are too many pieces of this puzzle still missing."

Ryan dumped the rest of his tea into the sink and headed for the door. "Listen, I have to scoot. My psych class starts in twenty minutes."

Disappointment flooded her, partly because they hadn't hit on a solution and partly because she didn't want him to go. "I thought you were going to help me."

"I am. Psych's my only class today. I'll be back at noon. We can check around town then. Someone may have seen Gram." Ryan paused. His eyes filled with concern. "You'll be okay?"

"Sure." Jennie half hoped he'd pick up the hesitation in her voice and ask her to go with him. He didn't.

"Make sure all the doors and windows are locked," he ordered, "and stay here until I get back."

Jennie thought about arguing with him. She didn't, even though this parental side of him annoyed her. She just bowed and said, "Yes, master," then shoved him out the door.

"I mean it, Jennie," he said, backing away.

"Okay, okay. I'll be careful."

Needing to do something to keep busy until Ryan came back, Jennie rewound the tape on the answering machine, hit the playback button, and listened to the messages again, thinking she might have missed something the night before. Who was the man who'd told Gram to come home, and why would he call Gram "Love"?

Could he be connected with the JB file in the computer? Is he a friend or a. . . ? *Don't be ridiculous, McGrady. She's a grandmother.*

Jennie frowned, remembering an article she'd seen somewhere called "Seniors: Finding Love the Second Time Around." *Okay, so it's possible.* The man had sounded nice, caring. She wished she had more than a voice. Maybe Gram had a picture. Or maybe she'd written about him in a journal.

Jennie raced up the stairs and into Gram's bedroom. The picture wall had about twenty photos on it. Gram and Grandpa's wedding picture, some baby pictures of Dad and Kate, graduation and wedding pictures . . . Uncle Kevin and Aunt Kate and Mom and Dad . . . a bunch of the grandkids.

Moving to her dresser, Jennie noticed a framed snapshot of Gram standing between two men in uniform. One was Grandpa. The other she didn't recognize. In fact, Jennie couldn't remember ever seeing the photo before. She eased the old brown-tone from the frame, wondering if names had been written on the back. The original notation was too faded to read, but written in clear black ink, like it had been done yesterday, were the words:

Found this in an old trunk . . . thought you might like it.

All my love . . . J.B.

Jennie put the picture back in the frame and carefully lowered it to the dresser. Whoever J.B. was, he'd known Gram and Grandpa for a long time.

Jennie picked up Gram's perfume and sprayed some on her wrist. *Wild Flowers.* The scent spread through the room, and Jennie could almost feel Gram there with her.

"What's going on, Gram?" she whispered. "Why is the sheriff after you? What have you done?"

Jennie was just about to go back downstairs when the phone rang. She started to answer, then stopped. It might be Mom or Aunt Susan. She ran downstairs and waited for the answering machine to pick up. "Jennie!" a frantic voice said after the beep.

Jennie grabbed the phone. "Lisa! Don't hang up. I'm here."

"Why didn't you call?" Lisa screeched. "I've been worried sick about you."

"I got in late and . . . besides, you were supposed to call me, remember?"

"I did. About ten times up until nine-thirty. Then the camp counselor locked the doors, so I couldn't get out to the pay phone."

"Why didn't you leave a message?" Jennie asked, remembering there were only two on the machine last night.

"The line was busy." Jennie remembered the after-shave lotion she'd smelled when she had arrived the night before and wondered if the phone-message burglar had been at it again.

"So, how's it going?" Jennie asked, pushing aside the burglar thoughts.

"Not great."

"What happened?"

"Your mom called here this morning and wanted to talk to you."

"What did you say?" Jennie felt her stomach drop. Nothing was working out like it was supposed to. Mysteries weren't supposed to have this many glitches in them. At least they never did in the books she'd read.

"I panicked. I told her you got sick last night and

couldn't get her on the phone, so you called Gram and she came to get you."

Jennie groaned. "You didn't."

"Well, what did you want me to tell her, that you'd eloped with some guy?"

"No. She'd never have believed that." Jennie sank into the chair beside the phone. "Why didn't you just tell her I was in the bathroom, or that I went for a walk?"

"It's not like I had a lot of time to rehearse, you know. Besides, you *are* sick—in the head."

Lisa sounded mad and Jennie didn't blame her. With the number of times she'd gotten Lisa into trouble, it was a wonder Lisa was still speaking to her. "Okay," Jennie said, "maybe it will work. What did Mom say?"

"She wanted to know what was wrong. I told her you had the flu and that Gram was going to stay in a hotel down here last night then head home today."

"Did she believe you?"

"I think so. Anyway, you'd better call her. She thinks you are on your way to Grams."

Jennie twisted the phone cord around her finger. "Lisa, I'm sorry about all this. It's just that I need to find out what's going on here. Besides, it wasn't all a lie. Gram *was* home." She filled her cousin in about everything except the diamonds.

"Do you want me to come down and help?" Lisa asked when Jennie had finished.

"No. But it might be a good idea if you went home. I could use you there to run interference. We can't let our moms know I'm down here alone. As long as they think Gram is back, they'll be okay. I'll call Mom and give her the same story you did. If I'm lucky she'll let me stay until the weekend. Maybe Ryan and I can solve this thing by then."

"Sounds like you and Ryan are becoming at item. Maybe I should come down *there* and run interference."

"Ryan is a *friend*."

"Right. He's also very male, very blond, and very gorgeous."

"Okay," Jennie admitted, "I think he's adorable, and he's got my heart racing. Satisfied?"

"Ha! It's about time. I was beginning to think you were anti-men."

"Because I'm not boy crazy like you?" Jennie retorted.

"I'm hurt."

"And I'm Madonna." They both cracked up on that one. Usually, when Lisa and Jennie got into this kind of banter, they'd go until they were both rolling around on the floor laughing. But nothing about the last few days had been normal.

"Ah, Lisa?" Jennie asked. "When are you going home?"

"As soon as I get my bags packed and have Mom come get me. What do you want me to do when I get home?"

"Whatever you have to—just keep them from coming down here."

"I don't like this, Jennie. Did it ever occur to you that if something has happened to Gram, you could be in danger too?"

"Don't be silly," Jennie answered with more confidence than she felt. "I'll be fine."

They talked for a few more minutes and hung up. Then Jennie called home. Michael answered. "Where's my mom?" she asked, trying hard to keep her voice calm.

"She's seeing a client. I'm watching Nick for her."

Jennie felt a fluttering of jealousy, and something else

she couldn't quite name. She didn't like the idea of Michael taking care of Nick. *And whose fault is that, McGrady? You're not there to do it.* Jennie shrugged the annoying feelings aside. She had too many other things going on to worry about Michael. Jennie told him the same story Lisa had about being sick and trying to call. She hoped they hadn't been home the night before.

"I'm sorry we weren't here for you, Jennie," Michael said.

Jennie let out the breath she'd been holding. "I think I should stay here for the rest of the week. I wouldn't want you guys to catch this." She coughed into the phone.

Liar, liar, pants on fire. Oh, shut up, Jennie told the persistent voice in her head. She didn't have a choice. She couldn't very well tell them the truth, could she?

"I don't know," Michael said. "I'll bet your mom will want you home."

"Couldn't you talk to her, Michael? I'm okay really. I'd just like to stay at Gram's for a few days."

"Okay. I'll talk to her and have her give you a call."

"Thanks." Then realizing she probably wouldn't be there, Jennie added, "I might be sleeping. If no one answers just have her leave a message." *O what tangled webs we weave* . . .

"Okay. Oh, and, Jennie, your mom and I have settled things on our wedding date."

"Really?" Jennie tried not to let her voice reflect her disapproval. Great. Another unanswered prayer. *God, don't you care about me at all? Couldn't you have made them wait until I found Dad?*

"Yes," Michael said. "And I think you'll be pleased by our decision."

Jennie took a deep breath. *Say it,* a voice inside ordered. *Tell him you'll never be pleased by any decision he and Mom make regarding marriage.*

Before she had a chance to respond, he went on. "We'd like *you* to set the date, Jennie."

"What?" Jennie couldn't have heard him right. "Me?"

"Well, it was my idea, actually. I know you're not happy about me being part of your family . . ."

Jennie winced. She hadn't meant to be so obvious. Or maybe she had.

"Anyway," Michael went on, "your mom and I decided we'd like to wait until you're able to give us your blessing."

Jennie couldn't say anything. Maybe it was the sound of his voice, or the realization that they really did care about how she felt. Anyway, she started crying.

"Jennie? You okay? I'm sorry, I guess I shouldn't have told you over the phone. It's just that I was anxious to let you know. Your mom and I prayed and prayed over this. We really wanted to do the right thing."

"You mean . . ." Jennie sniffled, ". . . if I say no, you won't marry Mom?"

Michael didn't answer right away and when he did, his voice was unsteady. Maybe he was crying too. "I wouldn't just be marrying your mom, Jennie, but your entire family. You and Nick are part of this, so we decided that if God really wants us to be together, everyone in the family has to be in agreement. The only thing I ask is that you wait a few days before giving us your answer. Think about it. Pray about it."

Jennie wanted to say no right then and there. She wanted to tell him she didn't have to think about it, only the words wouldn't come. All she could manage was a muffled "Okay . . ."

After saying goodbye, Jennie dropped the phone on the hook and walked away. She felt rotten. She'd lied and been a total brat toward Michael and Mom, and now they were letting her have a choice in whether or not they stayed together.

At first it had sounded like a great idea; now Jennie wasn't so sure. In fact the more she thought about it, the more angry she became. If she said no, everyone would be mad at her. If she said yes, she'd hate herself. Saying yes would be like giving up on Dad and Jennie couldn't do that.

Get a grip, McGrady. Even if it means everybody hating you, you have to say no. Besides, would they really listen to a sixteen-year-old? Probably not—but maybe you can hold them off until you find Dad.

And for that she needed Gram. Jennie closed her mind to Mom and Michael. She had to concentrate on finding Gram. The whole rest of her life depended on it. As soon as Ryan came back, they could launch into a full-scale investigation.

To keep busy, Jennie decided to wash the dishes. From the kitchen window she could practically see the whole block. Gram's house was set up like a lot of beach houses. The living room faced the ocean, and the kitchen faced the street side. Azalea and rhododendron blossoms splashed the yard with pink, lavender, and peach, giving it the impressionistic look of a Claude Monet painting. Birds flitted all over the feeder that hung from the big maple tree. Everything looked so sunny and bright—and normal—everything except for a shiny black Cadillac.

The driver cruised to the end of the block, turned around and came back. This time, instead of going past the house, he stopped on the other side of the street.

Jennie remembered what Ryan had said about the big guy driving off in a dark car and wondered if this was their intruder.

Even though her hands were soaking in hot sudsy water, Jennie felt cold. A chill started in her neck and shivered through her. When she realized he wasn't coming in, Jennie began to relax. He just sat there, like he was on some kind of surveillance. Maybe he was one of the jewel thieves. Maybe he knew Gram had the diamonds and was trying to catch her, or maybe he was waiting for her to leave so he could search the house.

Jennie wanted to get a closer look at him. But how?

Of course, the mailbox. She could walk out, nonchalantly check the box, maybe even strike up a conversation. "Hello," she could say. "Nice morning. Did you read about that diamond robbery the other day?" Okay, so she wouldn't talk to him. She just needed to get close enough to see his face and get the license number.

Yeah, right, the common sense part of her said, *and what if he grabs you?*

"He won't," Jennie reasoned aloud. "Not in broad daylight."

She took a deep breath, unbolted the door, and walked down the steps, pretending not to notice him.

It took forever to get to the mailbox. Her feet felt as if they'd been cast in concrete. She opened the box and pulled out a peach-colored envelope, just like the one Gram had sent to the school.

The sound of a car engine startled her. She dropped the letter and spun around. The black Cadillac had pulled away and raced down the street and around the corner. Relief and disappointment filled her. Just another minute or two and she would have seen him. *Another minute or two and you could have been dead.*

Jennie bent over to pick up the note she had dropped. It was then that she noticed the shiny black boots, the stone-washed jeans—and the hand reaching toward her.

11

"Let me get that for you."

Jennie screamed and jumped back . . . well actually, it was more like a squeak and a shuffle.

"I'm sorry, I didn't mean to frighten you."

He wasn't wearing his uniform, but Jennie had no trouble recognizing him. A guy like Joe Adams was hard to forget. He retrieved the envelope and handed it to her.

The breath she'd been holding went out in a swoosh. "Thanks." She shoved the letter into the back pocket of her jeans.

"Are you always this nervous around cops, or is it just me?" He smiled and Jennie had the distinct feeling he was flirting with her.

"I guess I'm still jumpy from last night. You and Sheriff Taylor scared me half to death."

"I'm sorry about that. The sheriff is taking this thing with your grandmother pretty hard. They've been friends a long time. You sure you haven't heard from her?"

His eyes were the color of melted chocolate, warm and sincere. Jennie almost told him the whole story. *He's a cop*, she reminded herself. *And he's after Gram. He's being nice so you'll trust him.* "I . . . I told you last night I haven't seen her."

"And you have no idea where she might be or where she's hidden the diamonds?"

Jennie couldn't lie to him. He'd know. Gram had told her once that police officers are trained to read people. Gram sure could. Jennie wondered how Joe was reading her. "Do you know Gram?" she asked.

Joe nodded. "We met when I first started working down here."

"Then you know she couldn't have stolen anything. She's missing. Someone could have kidnapped her. She could be in serious danger. You and Sheriff Taylor should be helping her, not trying to put her in jail."

Joe shook his head. "People aren't always what they seem." The sad look in his eyes told her he was speaking from experience.

"I know, but Gram . . . did you know she used to be a police officer?"

He nodded. "She's helped us crack a couple of cases. But cops, even good ones, can go bad." Joe straightened his shoulders and crossed his arms. "Tell you what," he said. His tone had changed along with his posture. "It may not look like it, but I'm on your side. The evidence against Mrs. McGrady is incriminating, maybe a little too incriminating. I'm not convinced she's guilty. But I need to talk to her—hear her side of it. So if you hear anything, see anything, that might help me find her, you let me know, okay?"

Jennie nodded. Joe seemed nice enough, but she wasn't convinced. Part of her wanted to trust him, but part of her held back. She could, however, tell him one thing. "There was a black Cadillac here a few minutes ago," Jennie said. "The driver sat here and watched the house for about ten minutes. I think it might be the same

106

guy who was in Gram's house last night."

Joe studied her for a moment, then took a small black notebook out of his front shirt pocket, flipped it open, and wrote in it. "I don't suppose you got a license number."

"No." The envelope had distracted her, but she didn't tell him that. Gram might have written it, and she wasn't about to show it to him.

Joe left, saying he'd check back later and reminding her to be careful and to call him if she found anything. She wouldn't, of course, but it didn't hurt to let him think she was cooperating.

Way to go, McGrady. Jennie scolded herself as she returned to the house. *Nancy Drew would have remembered to get the license number.* Drew was a fictitious character, she reminded herself.

Besides, she had noticed something even Drew might have missed. Joe Adams hadn't seemed surprised when Jennie mentioned the burglar having been at Gram's the night before. He acted as if it were old news. Ryan had reported the first one. But neither of them had mentioned the guy being in Gram's house before she had arrived. And the guy in the car. Joe had taken notes and seemed concerned, but why hadn't he asked for more information? And why had he happened by when she was about to get a look at the mysterious man in the black car? Were they working together?

Jennie poured a glass of orange juice and sat down at the kitchen table with her note pad. She pulled the envelope from her back pocket and tore it open.

I know you have the diamonds.

Jennie didn't recognize the handwriting. It slanted upward across the page and had jiggles in it, like Grandpa

Calhoun's did after he got Parkinson's Disease. Even with medication his writing was practically unreadable.

She didn't know anyone else with Parkinson's. Grandpa Calhoun certainly hadn't written it. He'd had a stroke a couple of years ago and lived in a rest home. Gram hadn't written it. So who? It could have been the man in the black car—or Joe—or maybe the man on the phone.

And why? Was the note for Gram? Or had it been meant to scare her?

He—or she—had written it on stationery exactly like Gram's. Was that a coincidence, or was it part of the message? Did the writer have Gram? Jennie didn't even want to think about that possibility.

You're not afraid, Jennie told herself. Actually, petrified was probably a better word. Maybe getting involved hadn't been such a good idea. Well, she was here now and for Gram's sake had to keep going.

She wrote the latest clues on her note pad and read through the list of clues again, hoping something would click. Gram had called the Johnsons and the sheriff—supposedly from Canada. But the day before she'd written Jennie a note and mailed it from Lincoln City.

A phone-message burglar wearing spicy aftershave, the watcher in a black Cadillac, a million dollars worth of diamonds hidden upstairs in a grocery bag, a warrant for Gram's arrest, and a note from someone who knew that Gram—or Jennie—had the diamonds.

None of it made much sense.

Jennie tore off her list of clues, crumpled the paper into a tight wad, and made a clean shot into the waste basket. Good thing Coach Haskel hadn't seen that. The basketball coach at Trinity called about once a month trying to recruit her for the girls' team. Every month she refused. Mom and Nick needed her more than the team did. At least they used to—before Michael came along. Before Michael. B.M. *Bad joke, McGrady. You ought to be ashamed of yourself. All this detecting is affecting your brain.*

Jennie tossed the pad aside and gulped down the rest of her juice. The digital clock on the microwave told her Ryan wasn't due back for another hour. Time enough, she decided, to call some of the people in Gram's phone directory. Maybe one of them could fill in the missing blanks.

Jennie got through the M's before finding anything helpful. Sherry Martin, who was a close friend of Gram's and an English teacher, told her that she had driven Gram to the airport on May fifteenth and was to pick her up on the twenty-third. "I got a call a few days later," Sherry said. "Helen said that she'd changed her plans and that I didn't need to pick her up after all. That's the last I've heard. I don't mind telling you I'm worried."

"Me too," Jennie said. She promised to call Sherry and let her know what developed.

Jennie felt pretty depressed by the time she got to the Z's. No one had seen Gram or knew where to find her. Jennie flipped through the remaining pages and on the last one saw a scribbled message. Actually it was just a string of letters, but Jennie had the feeling they were important. They began with *J.B.* The same initials she'd seen in Gram's computer file and on back of the picture upstairs. After them Gram had written *koecjoptsv*.

Jennie spent about ten minutes trying to make a word out of the letters but nothing made sense. "Maybe they're numbers," she murmured, assigning each letter a number, but that didn't make any more sense than the letters.

She was about to give up on the whole thing when her brain finally kicked in. This was Gram's telephone directory—what if the letters in her note matched the numbers on the telephone? Jennie punched in the numbers 563–256–7878. It rang. A recording told her to dial a one. It rang again.

"J.B. here."

It was the guy—the man with the James Bond voice who'd left a message on Gram's answering machine the night before.

"Hello! I say, is anyone there?"

"Ah . . . ," Jennie stammered. "Is Helen there?" Jennie had no idea why she'd asked him that, but it sure got his attention.

"Helen?" The voice boomed. "Now look here, who are you? Where did you get this number? Hello! Hello!"

Jennie hung up. She still didn't know who he was, but it felt good to have one piece of this crazy puzzle coming together. Her imagination conjured up all sorts of possibilities. He could be an editor. But that didn't fit. People didn't usually write a friend's or editor's name in code. Then Jennie thought about Grandpa McGrady and the uniforms. "Maybe he's a spy."

"Who's a spy?"

Jennie spun around, her elbow connecting with Ryan's midsection.

"Ow!" Ryan backed away, holding his stomach. "What was that for?"

"Sorry." Jennie rubbed her elbow. "But that's what you get for sneaking up on me. Did I hurt you?"

"I'll live." Ryan sprawled onto the sofa and rubbed his stomach. "So what's this spy business?"

Jennie showed him the coded message in Gram's book and told him about J.B.'s picture and the phone conversation.

"Well, whoever he is, one thing is certain. She doesn't want anyone to know about him."

"What has she gotten herself into, Ryan? Why can't Gram be a normal gray-haired grandmother who spends her days knitting, baking cookies, and rocking?" Like Grandma Rose. Mom's mother would *never* have become involved in something like this. Prim, proper, and poised. That described Mom *and* Grandma Rose. At least it had until her mother had flipped out over Michael.

Ryan shook his head. "Come on, Jennie. You love Gram the way she is. She's a McGrady—like you."

Jennie brightened. "You're right." She started to tell him about her trip to the mailbox and the note but decided not to. She figured he wouldn't have been too happy about it, especially when he'd been so adamant about her locking the doors and staying inside.

Fortified with hamburgers and sodas from McDonald's, they headed downtown to see if any of the locals had seen Gram. Bay Village wasn't a big town, just long. It sat on a rocky cliff with the ocean on one side and the coastal mountains on the other. Most of the fifty or so shops, restaurants, condominiums, and motels were located on the main highway. Their plan for the afternoon was to hit them all.

They parked Ryan's truck in a parking lot in the middle of town and walked up one side of the street and back on the other, stopping in every restaurant, store, motel, antique and gift shop on the way. No one could remember having seen Gram in the last month.

By three in the afternoon Ryan and Jennie were ready

111

to give up. They stopped at the Dairy Queen for ice cream, then took their cones across the street to a wayside park and sat on the thick concrete guardrail where they could watch the ocean smash into the rocks below.

"Ready to give up?" Ryan asked. "We could head down to Newport. Have dinner on the wharf and go agate hunting on the beach."

"Sounds great." The sky was a gorgeous shade of blue—almost the color of Ryan's eyes. The wind blew saltwater spray in their faces as the big waves splashed up over the railing and onto the sidewalk. "But we can't give up yet. We don't have too many places left." Jennie licked her chocolate-vanilla twist. "Maybe we could split up. You take the east side of the street, I'll take the west. I'll meet you at the parking lot behind the used book store at the end of town." Jennie smiled and added, "It shouldn't take us long. We'd still have time to go to Newport."

"Okay." Ryan crumpled his napkin and tossed it in a nearby trash can. "I'll come back and get the truck first . . . about twenty minutes?"

Jennie nodded and watched him jog across the street and into a gift shop. The thought of spending what was left of the afternoon and evening with Ryan had her heart doing cartwheels. She should have been cheering. Instead, she shivered. All of a sudden she felt uneasy. Jennie looked around, halfway expecting to see someone watching. There were a lot of tourists around, but no one seemed to be paying attention to her. No suspicious-looking character in a trench coat, or a slimy, sleezeball type in a stocking cap. And no black Cadillac. The only person she recognized was Sheriff Taylor driving by in his county sheriff's car. He waved.

Even though the sheriff was after Gram, seeing him drive by made her feel a little safer. Still, she took off across the street and didn't stop running until she got to the brick building, which housed an art gallery on one side and a souvenir shop on the other.

Ten minutes, three gifts shops, and a restaurant later, Jennie entered the used book store. It was a run-down, ramshackle old place that looked as if the only thing holding up the roof were the million or so musty-smelling books that filled it. Jennie scrunched down to pet the resident guard cat as it wound around her legs.

"Mrs. Stone?" she said to the gray-haired woman behind a counter littered with enough books to keep her reading for the next ten years.

The older woman peered over the top of her novel, one of those thick paperbacks with a mushy romance cover, and adjusted her glasses. "Jennie McGrady. It's been ages since you were here. I've got a bunch of Agatha Christie, a couple Nancy Drew, and some Mrs. Pollifax back there." She pointed in the general direction of a back room that housed her mystery collection. "And tell Helen I'm holding the Dorothy Sayers novel she wanted."

"Actually, Mrs. Stone, that's why I'm here," Jennie said. "I don't know where Gram is. I was hoping you'd seen her."

"Oh, my." She set her book down and leaned toward Jennie. "I knew all that chasing around would come to no good."

"Chasing around?"

"Oh, you know, always traveling, investigating, and writing those articles of hers. Last time I saw her she was researching cat burglars for a novel she was wanting to write."

"When was that?" Jennie asked, hoping she'd finally found a lead.

"Oh, honey, that was over three weeks ago. Before she left for Canada." Mrs. Stone reached into a cardboard box and thumbed through it. "Mmmm . . . Mc . . . McGrady . . . here it is. She was in on the tenth of May. Brought me in some trades and took out a pile of travel books, and about a half-dozen mysteries. Said she had some heavy readin' to do."

Jennie sighed. Gram always had heavy reading to do. "Are you sure she hasn't been in here in the last few days?"

"I'm afraid not, honey."

After thanking her, Jennie headed outside. The fresh ocean air felt good after the stale smell of too many moldy old books. She headed down the street toward the parking lot to wait for Ryan. The lot overlooked the ocean and provided parking for the small motel and the bed and breakfast next to it.

She'd gotten as far as the alley when she decided that meeting Ryan there hadn't been such a smart idea. The street was isolated and quiet—a little too quiet. The hair on the back of her neck prickled. Was someone watching her again?

She glanced around. Not a car or human in sight. Maybe it was just the cool air. The sky had clouded over and the wind had picked up. Jennie zipped up her jacket and stuffed her hands into its oversized pockets.

She shrugged off the uncomfortable sensation as a bad case of nerves, and ran the rest of the way to the parking lot. Jennie felt safer there in the open, near the motel. She watched the waves crash in, halfway hoping the ocean would throw a bottle full of answers up with the tide.

Jennie barely heard the engine over the roar of the surf. She waited for Ryan to join her so they could compare notes. Suddenly she caught the scent of spicy aftershave. A voice in her head shouted a warning. *Too late.*

A hand closed over her face. She struggled to get away. He tightened his grip, dragged her backward, and pushed her into the backseat of a black Cadillac.

12

Jennie was pushed to the floor of the car, face down. The door slammed. Tires screeched. She lifted her head and struggled to sit.

"Hold still!" The voice sounded hard and gravelly. He shoved her down again and yanked her arms behind her back.

"Ow!" she screamed. "Let me go! You're hurting me."

"Hey, take it easy. We're supposed to question her, not kill her." The second voice came from the front seat. Jennie was certain she'd heard the voice before, but couldn't place it.

The guy who had her pinned down grunted a response she couldn't hear over the roar of the motor. He tied her hands, then gagged and blindfolded her. When Jennie felt him move away, she kicked at him.

His yowl told her she'd connected. Jennie's success lasted about two seconds. That's how long it took him to tie her feet together.

Jennie stopped struggling then. She didn't want to think about what was going to happen, or how scared she was, or how much her ribs hurt from the hump in the floor. Instead, she tried to concentrate on where they were taking her.

When they pulled to a stop, Jennie heard voices and figured they were at the only traffic light in town. She vaguely remembered that the driver had taken a left turn off the side street where they'd abducted her. That meant they were heading north.

Oh, God, she prayed. *Please let Ryan know where I am. Please let him find me.*

Jennie wasn't too sure it would do any good to pray or that God would answer. With the way she had been acting lately she probably didn't deserve His help. But she figured it wouldn't hurt to ask.

They were moving again. A few minutes later the driver accelerated. Jennie pictured the 55 MPH speed-limit sign at the edge of town. She counted. At one hundred the driver slowed and made a left turn. They were headed toward the beach. The car bumped over several potholes, which meant they were probably on one of the private roads that fingered off the coast highway into residential areas. Her heart rate quickened with hope. They couldn't be too far from Gram's.

They stopped again. "Get her into the house. I'll put the car in the garage and call the boss." When Jennie heard the driver's voice again, a picture of a man formed in her mind. *Joe Adams.* But that was impossible. Joe was the sheriff's deputy, not a kidnapper. Maybe he was working undercover. *Or maybe he's one of them.*

What was it he'd said? "Even good cops can go bad." Had he been talking about himself? Jennie wanted to hear his voice again to make sure. Unfortunately, the men weren't in a talkative mood. King Kong hauled her out of the car and slung her over his shoulder.

"Dan!" the guy she thought might be Joe yelled. King Kong stopped and turned. "Be careful with the kid."

So the monster had a name. Somehow that knowledge gave her strength. She was dealing with a person—a known entity. Maybe she had a chance.

Dan grunted, swung back around, and carried her inside and up a flight of stairs. It had the musty smell of a place that hadn't been used in years.

"Uhhh!" Jennie's muffled scream broke the silence as he threw her off his shoulders. She landed on something padded and springy—probably a mattress.

He rolled her onto her stomach, grabbed her feet, and tied them to what felt like the bed frame.

Jennie screamed again.

"I'd save my voice if I were you, kid. You're going to need it to tell us where the old lady hid the diamonds."

When the door closed, Jennie's protests turned to sobs. She shouldn't have gotten involved. What if they used drugs to make her talk? Or tortured her? She knew too much . . . except she really didn't know where Gram was. They might find out about the diamonds, but that was all.

Jennie relaxed a little then and tried not to cry. She took a deep breath to calm herself, then wished she hadn't. She nearly gagged on the smell of the rotting mattress pressed against her nose. She rolled onto her back, twisting tight the rope that held her feet. There had to be a way out of this. *Think, McGrady.* If she could see, maybe she could figure out how to work the ropes loose.

By pressing into the mattress and moving her head up and down, she managed to loosen the blindfold. Jennie rose to a sitting position and shook it off her head. She'd been right about one thing, the house was old. The bed had an antique brass frame and a stained, lumpy mattress.

A bare light bulb hung from a frayed cord in the middle of the ceiling. She straightened and looked out the window. Jennie knew this town. Maybe she could spot a familiar house or landmark. A giant maple tree blocked most of the view. Discouraged, she sank back against the mattress, wincing as a sharp pain coursed through her shoulder. The muscles in her arms were already cramping from being tied behind her back.

It was nearly dark when Jennie heard someone coming up the stairs. The door slammed open. Two men stood in the doorway. They blocked the light from the hall so she couldn't see their faces.

The shorter of the two flipped on the light switch and came toward her. She had guessed right. The driver was Joe.

"I thought you blindfolded her!" he yelled.

"I did." Dan looked more like a linebacker than a gorilla, about six inches taller than Joe, and twice as wide. He scooped up the blindfold and handed it to Joe.

Jennie closed her eyes. *You're dead meat, McGrady.* She'd read enough mysteries to know what would happen next. She could identify them. They'd never let her walk out of there alive.

Joe stepped up to the bed and untied the gag. "Why don't you make this easy on all of us," he said. "Just tell us where the diamonds are."

"I don't know." Jennie hoped they couldn't read the truth in her eyes. Her throat felt rough and dry. "Could I have some water?"

"Sure," Dan said. "You can have anything you want—after you tell us where to find the ice."

"I told you, I don't know."

"You're being too easy on her," King Kong growled. "I'll make her talk."

"There's no need," Joe said firmly. "The boss has other plans. He figures the McGrady woman will be only too happy to talk when we tell her we have her granddaughter."

"What do you mean?" Jennie gasped. "Do you know where Gram is?"

Ignoring her questions, Dan argued, "Even if she talks we can't let the kid go. She can ID both of us."

Joe frowned. "Looks that way," he mumbled. Joe put the gag back over her mouth. As they left, Joe turned out the light and closed the door behind him.

Her life was over. Jennie felt as though they'd shut off the light inside her and closed the door to her future. She'd really messed things up. Gram would do whatever they wanted to keep her safe. Jennie could only hope they hadn't already gotten to her.

Somewhere inside, though, Jennie knew that was only wishful thinking. Gram was mixed up in this diamond robbery somehow. Had she been part of a sting operation to break up a ring of jewel thieves and gotten caught in the middle? Had she hidden the diamonds and sent Jennie a card because she was afraid they'd capture her and . . .

Could that be why whoever sent the anonymous note used Gram's stationery—to tell Jennie they had Gram? Jennie closed her eyes. She didn't want to think about any more possibilities.

A street light managed to sneak through some of the leaves of the tree outside the window, throwing wavy splotches of light into the room. Downstairs a door slammed. A car started. Then silence.

Jennie concentrated on the light and tried hard not to

think about being alone . . . about Gram . . . about dying.

Sometime later, she heard noises downstairs again. They were back. She smelled the food about the same time Joe came in with a tray. He flipped on the light, untied her hands, and released the gag. "Thought you might be getting hungry."

Jennie rubbed at her wrists and arms, trying to get some circulation back. They felt disconnected until the tingling started.

"Your hands hurt?"

Jennie nodded. "Cold."

Joe took her hands in his and rubbed them between his warm ones. She almost said, "What's a nice guy like you doing in a dump like this?" when it dawned on her. Joe wasn't a nice guy. He was a crook—a kidnapper. Jennie jerked her hands back.

Joe stood and ran a hand through his dark hair. "You better eat your soup while it's hot."

She ate. It was chicken noodle from a can, but it tasted good and warm and it soothed her throat. Tears gathered in her eyes and dropped into the soup. She didn't bother to wipe them away. They'd have just come back anyway.

"Is the soup that bad?"

Jennie didn't look up at him. "It needed salt." She half smiled at her response, wondering if it was normal to joke around when you're about to die, or if it was a sign that she'd totally lost her mind.

Joe didn't respond. He just sat there watching her eat.

If only she hadn't insisted on going to the bookstore. If only she hadn't gone to the parking lot to wait. She could have been having a nice dinner with Ryan and been hunting agates on the beach. Maybe he would have kissed

121

her good-night like he had the night before. Now she'd never see him again.

When Jennie had finished the soup and had taken a few sips of the grape juice he'd brought, she pushed the tray away. She imagined herself throwing it at him and running from the room. But even in her imagination she couldn't get her feet untied fast enough to get away.

"I need to use the bathroom." Maybe she could get out through the window.

"Sure." He untied her feet and ushered her out the door and down the hall. "Dan's standing guard outside, so don't get any ideas about running."

After flushing the toilet Jennie turned on the faucet and took advantage of the noise to pry up the window. She managed to open it about two inches. When the water in the toilet stopped running, she gave her hands a quick wash and left the room. Next time she'd open it a little farther—if there was a next time.

After he tied her up again, Jennie stared at the swaying, mottled light on the ceiling for a long time. She wasn't sure how she managed it, but she must have slept because the next thing she knew it was light. Fuzzy from sleep, Jennie wondered where she was. Her entire body felt as if she'd been used for a punching bag. The pain brought everything into focus.

She was still trussed up like a rodeo calf. Someone had covered her with a blanket and put a pillow under her head. Probably Joe. Jennie thought about the warmth she'd seen in his brown eyes when he'd talked with her at the mailbox. She found it hard, even after the kidnapping, to think of him as a criminal. He just didn't seem the type.

I guess you're a lousy judge of character, McGrady. Jennie heard steps on the stairs just before the door opened. Dan stalked across the room, untied her legs from the bed, and scooped her up into his arms. "Someone wants to talk to you."

He carried her downstairs and set her in a chair before taking the gag off. Joe held the phone against his chest. "It's your grandmother. Just tell her you're okay."

"Gram?" Jennie's voice cracked.

"Jennie!" Gram sounded angry at first, then her voice softened. "Are you okay, dear? They haven't harmed you?"

"I'm all right," Jennie answered, her voice shaky. "Gram, don't tell them anything. They're not going to let me go. Don't . . ."

Dan slapped the gag over her mouth.

"Jennie's fine," Joe told Gram. "Cooperate and we'll let her go." Joe put his hand over the mouthpiece. "Get her out of here."

King Kong threw Jennie over his shoulder again. She doubted that her screaming did anything, except make him more annoyed, and make her throat more sore than it had been before.

Dan dumped her back on the bed, tied her down, and left the room. This time she didn't cry. She kicked the bed frame, hoping maybe her fury would break the dilapidated thing apart. No such luck. All she managed to break was her foot—at least that's what it felt like.

The next few hours were torture. The ropes had scraped her wrists raw. Her muscles cramped every time she moved. As much as her body hurt, Jennie's heart hurt even more. They had Gram. They'd probably been holding her captive for days, trying to force her to tell them where she'd hidden the diamonds.

And Jennie had played right into their hands. She thought about telling them where the diamonds were hidden if they'd let Gram go. But what good would that do? As soon as they got the diamonds, they'd kill them both.

It looked as if her only option was to get free, then come back and follow Joe and Dan, and hope they led her to their boss and to Gram. Once she knew where they were she could call Sheriff Taylor. Unfortunately, her plan hinged on one minor detail. She needed to escape.

Much later, around lunchtime Jennie figured, Joe brought in a peanut butter and jelly sandwich and a glass of milk.

"My last meal?" Jennie's sarcastic comment came out in a whisper.

Joe frowned. "You've been watching too many detective movies."

"You mean you're not going to kill me?"

"Just eat." Joe walked over to the window and peered outside. The frown on his forehead deepened.

Jennie looked past him and saw a white patrol car through the tree branches. A glimmer of hope fluttered through her. Out on the street, Sheriff Taylor was standing beside his car talking to someone. He was probably making his rounds. If she could just get his attention. . . . Jennie opened her mouth to scream for help.

Joe slapped his hand against her mouth and pulled her against him. She bit his hand and jabbed her elbow into his stomach. He let out a muffled curse, pressed her face into the pillow, and fell on top of her.

"Hold still," Joe commanded as he slipped the gag back on and retied her hands. "Look, I'm sorry you got dragged into this, Jennie, but you're in it now, and it'll go a whole lot better for you if you cooperate."

After making sure she couldn't cause him any more trouble, Joe left, taking with him Jennie's half-eaten sandwich and the glass of milk.

It was dark before she saw either of the men again. Judging from the darkness and the way her stomach was growling, it had to have been way past dinner. She heard footsteps on the stairs, then in the hall.

Dan burst into the room, and he hadn't come to feed her.

"Time for you and me to take a little walk." As he reached over to untie her legs, Jennie froze. He had a gun tucked in the waistband of his pants, the handle pressed into a stomach that looked like a stuffed pillow. "Only for you," he sneered, "it's going to be a one-way trip."

13

Jennie and Dan met Joe at the bottom of the stairway. "Where do you think you're going?" Joe snapped.

"To dispose of a little unnecessary baggage."

"That wasn't part of the plan. Take her back upstairs."

"The boss changed his mind. You got a problem with that?"

"Yeah. You shoot her and every law enforcement agency in the country will be after us."

Dan snorted. "Who said anything about shooting her? This little gal is gonna take a walk out on the rocks by the beach. She gets too close to the edge . . . oops. It's all over. No bullets, and if we're lucky, no body . . . at least not till we're outta here."

For a second, Jennie thought Joe would stop him. Then he shrugged and stepped aside.

"No!" Jennie screamed through the gag. *Joe, don't let him hurt me*. Dan poked her in the back with his gun.

Jennie glanced behind her. Joe stood in the doorway, his arms folded across his chest. "Hey," Joe called. Hope exploded inside her. *He's not going to let Dan kill me after all*. Joe added, "If you want her death to look like an accident, you'd better untie her hands and get rid of the gag."

Dan snorted and loosened the ropes on her wrists, but left the gag in place. She guessed he didn't want her making too much noise until they got away from the houses. Jennie massaged the aching muscles in her arms and shoulders and turned to make one last plea for Joe to save her. He was gone. "Let's go." Dan pushed her on ahead of him.

Might as well give it up and accept your fate, McGrady, part of her conceded. *You've run out of options.* Jennie struggled against the hopelessness. She didn't give up easily. But then she didn't have many choices when a guy the size of a redwood was holding a loaded gun at her back.

Jennie's legs and feet, stiff from being tied up so long, felt disconnected. She stumbled twice on the gravel driveway, but her clumsiness didn't stop Dan. He simply yanked her up and set her back down on her feet again.

They turned from the lighted driveway to the trees. His flashlight bobbed up and down on the narrow path. Jennie tried not to think about the end of the walk. Or the trail winding through the woods. The cliff. The rocks. The dark swirling water that would soon be her grave. She began praying, *God, if you're really up there, I could use a little help. And if I have to die, please take care of Mom and Nick . . .*

"What the . . ." WHAM! A heavy thud interrupted Jennie's prayer. She glanced back. Dan was sprawled out on the ground. His gun had landed at her feet. She scooped it up, stuffed it in her jacket pocket, and ran.

The only light Jennie had came from slivers of moonlight sneaking through the tall firs. Branches slashed at her face and arms as she wove through the woods. Her lungs burned and felt as though they'd burst.

When she was sure she'd outrun Dan, Jennie pressed herself against a tree. She pulled off the gag and hauled in as much air as her lungs would hold. Blood pounded through her body like a sledge hammer. She listened for footsteps, but all she could hear was the wind stirring the leaves above her head, the pounding surf, the sound of her own ragged breathing, and her heart thudding in her chest. Relief surged through her. She'd lost him.

Her hope for the future didn't last long. She heard a rustling noise in the bushes behind her. Heavy footsteps beat the ground. Jennie pushed off from the tree and started running again. She'd gotten only a few steps when someone grabbed her around the waist and pulled her into the thick undergrowth.

"Shhh," a familiar voice whispered in her ear. "It's me."

Jennie collapsed against him. "Get down." Ryan dropped to the ground and pulled her with him. They flattened out on the forest floor and waited. She closed her eyes and willed her body to become part of the thick moss and rotting wood. Every snapping twig, every foot-step, and every swoosh of the branches wound her nerves tighter and tighter until she wanted to scream. Finally, the thrashing faded.

"He's searching the other side. Let's go." Ryan helped her up and tugged her forward. They'd gone only a few yards when they stumbled onto another path.

"Where are we?" Jennie whispered.

"Just above Smugglers' Cove."

"How did . . ."

"Later." Ryan grabbed her hand and took off again.

The forest path dead-ended at the ocean. A metal cable guarded the hundred-foot drop-off. Ryan let go of her hand, swung under the cable, and started down. Jennie followed. They didn't talk. Didn't have to. They had climbed down to Smugglers' Cove at least fifty times.

When they got to the bottom, Ryan took her hand again. "We'll hide in the cave I found. We should be safe there." They ran along a stretch of sand to an outcropping of rocks.

"The tide's coming in. We'd better hurry." They raced the waves and beat all but one. Just as they crossed the last stretch of beach a wave crashed against Jennie's legs and nearly knocked her down. She reached up and caught Ryan's hand. "You okay?" he asked, hauling her out of the icy water.

No, I'm not okay! she wanted to cry. Instead she nodded, trying to ignore the chill seeping into her bones and the sharp sting of salt water burning into her rope-burned ankles. *Keep going, McGrady,* Jennie ordered. *You can't give up now.* Jennie concentrated on getting her feet to move and started climbing again.

She didn't see the cave until Ryan wedged himself between two tall boulders and disappeared. "Come on." He snaked his arm out and pulled her in.

"I can't see a thing," she whispered, tightening her grip on his hand.

"Yeah. And I don't have a flashlight . . . or matches." Ryan drew her forward a few feet, then turned her around. "You can sit here. There's a rocky ledge behind you—makes a kind of chair. It's dry."

"I'm not." Jennie sat on the ledge and wrung the excess water out of her jeans. Somehow the climb and the safety of the cave had lessened the chill, but she shivered anyway. A narrow haze of moonlight filtered into the cave's entrance. Enough light to take the edge off the darkness, but not enough to really see.

"How did you find me?" Jennie asked as Ryan settled beside her.

"I was coming to pick you up when this black Cadillac tore out of the side street where I was supposed to meet you. I pulled into the lot. When you didn't show up I got worried. I went to the bookstore, and Mrs. Stone told me you'd been there and left."

"And I was waiting for *you* when I heard a car pull up behind me. I thought it *was* you. Talk about stupid! I just stood there and let them kidnap me. I should have run." Jennie shivered again.

Ryan put his arm around her. "Don't be so hard on yourself. You couldn't have known. Anyway, I doubt you'd have gotten far."

"I suppose . . . but . . . what did you do when you realized I wasn't coming?"

"I was pretty sure they'd gotten you, but by then the car was gone. I called Sheriff Taylor." Ryan sighed. "He was no help at all. Said I couldn't file a missing person's report for twenty-four hours. Then he laughed and told me he'd seen you running down the street earlier and that I'd probably just been stood up."

"The creep. You don't think he's involved in this do you?"

"I doubt it. He's getting ready to retire. My dad says he's just getting old and lazy. Anyway, with him looking for Gram, I didn't want to tell him too much, so I decided I'd try to find you on my own. I must have driven down every street in and out of town. Late this afternoon, I was about ready to give up and talk to the sheriff again when

130

I saw the car pull out of the gas station. I followed it."

"Where were they hiding me?"

"It's the old Wakefield house. It's only a couple blocks from Gram's and has been empty for about five years. I went home and took the back way here through the trees. Tried to figure out how to get to you. When the big guy brought you out, I saw my chance."

"So you tripped him and rescued me. That was so brave."

"Well, actually, I didn't trip him. I went around and came in from the beach side and was waiting for a chance to distract him when he fell. Ah . . . actually, I think someone . . . that is . . . I could have sworn I saw a shadow in the trees just before he went down. But . . . it was probably just my imagination."

"Well, thanks anyway," Jennie said, wondering if the shadow might have been Joe. She dismissed the thought as wishful thinking. Dan had probably just stumbled over a root. Jennie leaned her head against Ryan's shoulder. "You saved my life. He was going to kill me."

"I figured that, but why?"

"I can identify them." She told Ryan about them kidnapping her to get Gram to tell them where she'd hidden the diamonds.

"What a mess. It's hard to believe Adams would be involved in something like this. He's supposed to take over when Sheriff Taylor retires."

Jennie nodded, then realized Ryan couldn't see her. "I know, but facts are facts. Joe is involved, all right. I got the feeling he didn't want me to get hurt, but still . . . from the way he acted when the sheriff came by, I have no doubt. I wish I knew what to do next."

"Me too."

"Do you think it's safe to go back to Gram's?" Jennie asked.

"No. Those guys aren't going to give up easily. They're probably watching her house."

"We can't stay here."

"I don't know . . . maybe we should." Jennie felt Ryan move away.

"Where are you going?" She jumped up and grabbed for him, but got only a handful of air. "Ryan?" she yelped, not even trying to hide the panic in her voice.

Ryan pulled her into his arms. "I'm sorry, I didn't mean to scare you."

Jennie leaned her head against his chest. She seemed to be operating on two tracks. Ryan felt warm and comforting. But inside, fear raged, sending jolts of panic through her. "I wish I could see something. I've always hated the dark."

"Then you won't like my next suggestion."

"What?"

"I want you to stay here while I sneak back to my house for food, matches, and blankets. We need supplies, and you need dry clothes."

"I'll go with you."

"It's too dangerous. Besides, they're looking for you, not me. Even if they spot me, they probably won't do anything. They're used to seeing me around." Ryan tightened his grip. "You'll be safe here. I'll only be gone ten, fifteen minutes max."

"No, don't . . ."

He kissed her. The warm feel of his lips over hers had just begun to spread through her like melted butter when he disappeared through the cave opening. Jennie hurried after him and stopped at the entrance, then watched him

132

scamper over the rocks as if he knew them all by heart. He probably did. When he was gone she sat just outside the cave and gazed into the starry night. A smile curled her lips.

You're a nut case, McGrady, she said to herself. *Totally insane. You've been kidnapped, bound and gagged, held at gunpoint, threatened with death, and nearly drowned. Your jeans are soaked and your legs half-frozen, and you're grinning over a silly little kiss.*

A rustling noise in the trees above sobered her fast. She backed quietly into the cave. Footsteps thundered overhead, then stopped.

"I could have sworn I saw someone sitting out here."

"Give it up, Dan. We've lost her."

Great. They were still after her. As a deputy, Joe probably knew this area. What if he knew about the cave?

"The boss isn't gonna like this," Dan said.

"Maybe not, but it doesn't make a whole lot of difference."

"What if the kid goes to the cops?"

"That's not going to get her very far, is it?" Joe answered. "Who's going to believe her? We've set up an airtight case against the McGrady woman. By the time anyone figures it out, we'll be out of the country."

Unfortunately, he was right. Sheriff Taylor would never believe her, especially since she was the granddaughter of a fugitive. And with the diamonds in Gram's house, going to the authorities now would make things worse for Gram.

"Let's go," Joe said. "We'd better report in."

"You do that," Dan said. "I'll double back to the McGrady house and see if the kid went back there."

The voices and footsteps faded. Jennie's knees buckled. She leaned against the wall to hold herself up. Had they really gone? Or was it just a trick? Her jeans were only wet to her thighs, but the cold had seeped into her entire body. A shiver shook through her. Jennie stuffed her hands into her jacket pockets. Her hand connected with the gun.

Jennie had never held a real gun before. The closest she'd ever come to shooting anyone was with a squirt gun. She cradled the cool metal and slipped her finger around the trigger. A real gun with real bullets. Her mother hated guns. Dad sometimes wore one under his jacket. She shuddered, remembering the hardness of it when he'd hugged her that last time. She tried to imagine what Dad and Gram would do. She wasn't certain. The only thing she did know was that she would die before letting them kidnap her again. Jennie swallowed hard and made a decision. If they came back she'd be ready.

A few minutes later Jennie heard footsteps again. A shadow blocked out the sliver of moonlight. Jennie backed against the cave wall, lifted the gun from her pocket, and took aim.

14

"Jennie?" Ryan's voice exploded in the darkness.

Jennie let out the breath she'd been holding and dropped the gun back in her pocket. She clamped a hand over her mouth to stifle the scream that had risen to her throat. Jennie felt relieved and at the same time horrified by what she might have done. The first chance she got she intended to throw the thing in the ocean.

Ryan flipped on a flashlight and directed it at her. "Are you okay?"

"Yeah. Never been better." She pushed away from the wall that had been holding her up. "I enjoy being scared out of my mind every few minutes. I thrive on the adrenalin rush a hefty dose of fear gives me. Of course, the biggest thrill I've had all day was coming this close to shooting you."

Ryan frowned but didn't reply. He turned the flashlight beam on the stuff he'd brought and started unpacking. *Nice going, McGrady. What an idiot. It was your idea to use the gun for protection, and now you're blaming him.* Ryan was the last person she should have been mad at.

"I'm sorry. I didn't mean to snap at you." Jennie wove her fingers through her hair. "I . . . I was scared. Joe and Dan were here. They were standing so close I could hear

135

every word they said. I was afraid they'd come back. The gun . . . I couldn't let them . . ." Jennie's words sounded as fragmented as she felt.

"I know. They were here when I came back. I couldn't see them very well. I . . ." He cleared his throat. "I was afraid they'd found you."

Tension stretched between them, like an overinflated balloon. Jennie wanted him to drop everything and take her in his arms—to tell her everything would be all right. But he didn't.

"Here." Ryan handed Jennie his flashlight. "Hold this while I unpack."

Somehow having something to do helped pull Jennie's scattered thoughts and fears into a more manageable form. While Ryan pulled out food, clothes, and whatever else he had in his backpack, Jennie examined the cave. Except for a deep jagged crevice on one side, the cave had the shape of a small dome—about ten feet in diameter. Since Ryan could stand without slouching, Jennie figured the uneven ceiling to be around six feet—seven in some places.

Ryan spread out two sleeping bags in the center of the cave, one on either side of the supplies. Watching him work sent all the butterflies in her stomach flying again. "Ah . . . maybe staying here isn't such a good idea."

Ryan straightened. "Why not? Oh . . . I see. You're worried that I might want to . . ."

"No," Jennie interrupted and turned away from him so he wouldn't see the flush in her cheeks. "Well, maybe. I mean . . . things aren't like they used to be between us. We're not just friends anymore and it's . . . more complicated."

"I probably shouldn't have kissed you. Jennie, you

don't have to worry about me. It won't happen again."

"No. I mean . . . I'm glad you kissed me. And I'm not worried . . . not exactly." Jennie started chewing on the end of her hair then spit it out. Yuk. She hadn't done that since the sixth grade. "This is so embarrassing," she said, twisting back to face him. "I can't believe I'm having this conversation with you."

"Me either." Ryan stuffed his hands in his pockets and grinned. "Ah . . . look, I don't know about you, but these wet jeans are about to drive me nuts." He knelt beside a pile of clothes and extracted two pairs of jeans. "These are for you. They're mine. Might be a little big, but they're dry. You can change in here. I'll go outside."

Funny how a dry pair of Levis can change your whole outlook on life. Okay, so maybe it wasn't just the jeans. Jennie had also picked the moss and tree limbs out of her hair and pulled it back into a ponytail.

When Ryan came back in, they sat on the stone chair and ate the tuna sandwiches and nacho chips he'd brought.

"This is really good, Ryan. I'm starved. Thanks."

"Don't thank me, thank Mom."

"She knows we're spending the night out here?" Jennie nearly choked. She, Ryan, Lisa, and Kirk had often camped out on the beach during their stays with Gram. She'd never thought anything about it before, but things were different now.

"Relax. She knows *I'm* camping out. I decided not to tell her about you. And not for the reason you think. I just didn't want her to be able to tell Joe where you were."

That makes sense—the less she knows the better, Jennie decided. "I just wish we knew more. I still can't understand what part Gram is playing in all this."

137

"Maybe if we knew who they were working with we'd be able to put it all together."

Jennie swallowed a bite of sandwich and reached in the bag for a handful of chips. "You know what's so weird about this?"

"What?"

"The way nothing makes sense. I mean . . . Gram isn't a thief, but she's got both the crooks *and* the law after her. And there's Joe. I still can't picture him as one of the bad guys. He seemed so sincere. It really bugs me to think I could be so wrong about someone."

Ryan shrugged. "You were wrong about me."

"What do you mean?"

Jennie brushed the cheesy powder from the chips off her hands.

"Well, all these years you've thought of me as being your good old buddy, Ryan. The innocent next-door neighbor."

"You're not?"

He shook his head and raised his arm to cover his nose and mouth. "I've had you fooled, haven't I?" Ryan's voice dropped to a low, husky growl. "Never once did you suspect that under all these good looks lurks an alien being. Once a month when the moon is full I come to this cave and turn into . . ." Ryan dropped his arm to reveal a mouthful of fangs. He lunged at Jennie. "A werewolf!"

Jennie wasn't sure why she found him so funny. Could have been the tension . . . all she'd been through in the last forty-eight hours. She squealed and collapsed in a heap of giggles.

Ryan hauled her off the floor and onto the ledge beside him. "I wasn't that funny."

"No," she hiccupped, holding her side. "You were

awful." She gave his arm a playful punch. The tension between them had evaporated and they were acting like comfortable old friends again. Well, not *just* friends.

"Thanks," she said, leaning against him.

"For what?"

"For making me see that, except for liking each other a little more, things haven't changed that much between us. Hic . . ."

"Does that mean I can kiss you again?"

"No way . . . hic . . . not with those fangs in your mouth. Besides, I can't stop hiccupping."

Ryan pulled out his Dracula dentures and stuffed them back in his pack. "Hmm . . . I think I've read somewhere that kissing cures hiccups."

"Nice try. I think I'll stick to drinking upside down and holding my breath."

"Upside down . . . you're kidding, right?"

"No. Seriously. Gram showed me. Hic . . . Got any water?"

Ryan retrieved a canteen from his gear and handed it to her. "This I've got to see."

Jennie placed her lips on the opposite side of the canteen, bent over at the waist, held her breath and drank until she thought she would explode. She straightened and handed back the canteen. "There." She took a deep breath and let it out. "I'm cured."

Ryan chuckled. "Well, so much for *my* theory." Ryan put his arm around her shoulders, and Jennie rested her head against his shoulder.

She didn't want to think about anything except Ryan. Unfortunately, Jennie's mind was determined to move onto other more pressing matters.

She thought about Gram and this complex mystery

they had stumbled into. There were so many questions whirling around in her head and so few answers. "Are we ever going to figure out what's happened to Gram?" she asked.

"Let's not think about it now. It's late. We should get some sleep."

"You're right. I'm bushed." Jennie yawned and stretched. They took turns going outside to brush their teeth and wash up. After they'd crawled into their sleeping bags, Ryan switched off the flashlight.

Jennie lay there for a long time listening to his deep, steady breathing. Her mind ran through all the things that had happened in the last two weeks. She thought about Mom and Michael, Nick—and about Dad . . . and Gram.

Jennie was desperate to find Gram. Not so much because she wanted her to help find Dad, she realized, but because Jennie couldn't imagine life without her. She still wanted to look for Dad, of course, but the most important thing now was for Gram to survive.

Jennie realized something else too. She wasn't mad at Mom or Michael anymore. She wasn't certain when that change had happened. Maybe it had something to do with Michael telling her she could set their wedding date. Or maybe it was being with Ryan and discovering how good it felt to be held and kissed and feel loved. Maybe Mom needed someone like Michael in her life. "Oh, Dad," Jennie whispered. "Why couldn't you have come home before she met him?"

"Did you say something?" Ryan mumbled.

"I was just thinking about my Dad."

"Hmmm."

"Everybody thinks I've got some kind of emotional

140

hang-up." Remembering what the counselor had said, she added, "That I'm in denial."

"Hmmm."

"I'm not. I mean . . . it's like there's a door open between Dad and me. Not like when Grandpa McGrady died. That was hard too, but different. Gram and I have talked about it. She feels the same way. She says with Dad it's like a book without an ending. Neither one of us is ready to put it down until it's finished. I'm going to ask her to help me look for him this summer. Did I tell you that?"

Ryan didn't answer. Jennie rolled onto her back and stared at a ceiling she couldn't see. Tears welled up in her eyes and spilled into her hair. She was beginning to understand why Mom might want to marry Michael. She could even understand why her mom thought Dad was dead. Jennie just hoped her mom wasn't right. Maybe if Dad had given up his work like Mom wanted . . . spent more time at home. If he'd known the pain his job was going to cause, would it have made a difference? Would Dad make the same choice again?

Jennie turned back over and wiped her face with her sweatshirt sleeve. She listened to the ocean crashing against the rocks below and tried to imagine the water beating against all the confusion and hurt inside her. She let the sounds soothe away the wrinkles in her mind like the waves washed the sand, leaving it clear and clean.

Jennie must have slept because the next thing she heard was a chorus of gull cries and a faint scratching noise. Dawn sneaked slivers of light through the cave opening. Ryan scooted out of his sleeping bag and scrambled to his feet. "C'mon, sleepyhead," he said. "You have a choice of dry cereal or dry cereal for breakfast."

Jennie groaned. She tried to shut out the light—and Ryan—by burying deeper into her sleeping bag. She was just beginning to remember where she was and why she was there. The sleeping bag was warm and cozy and safe, and Jennie wished she could stay there forever.

A loud groan and a thud brought her fully awake. Jennie scrambled out of her sleeping bag and crawled toward the sound. Ryan lay crumpled near the cave's entrance. A trickle of blood oozed from a cut on his temple. Frightened, Jennie peered out the opening. No one. *Did he trip?* She put an ear to Ryan's chest and felt it rise and fall—heard the strong steady beat of his heart. She had to get something to stop the bleeding.

Jennie dug around in Ryan's pack, found a red bandana, and pressed it to his head. It was then she felt it, a presence. She chanced a quick look behind and wished she hadn't. Even in daylight the rear of the cave was black. Had Dan and Joe come back? Had they hurt Ryan?

You're paranoid, McGrady, she told herself. *If someone had been here you'd have heard voices. You'd have seen them. He fell—probably hit his head on a rock.*

Still, she had to be sure. Jennie slowly reached for the flashlight and heard a swishing sound behind her, like the sound of cloth against cloth. Jennie flipped on the light and spun around. Her arm connected with a solid mass. The light flew out of her hand and crashed to the floor.

A hand gripped her shoulder. She felt a sharp sting in her neck. Jennie jerked free. Almost immediately she felt the burning sensation travel from her neck to her brain, throwing her into slow motion. She'd been drugged. *Run, McGrady. Get away. To the opening.* Her mind sent orders her legs couldn't obey. Her knees buckled and pitched her forward.

"Easy now . . ." Strong arms lifted her as though she were a small child. "You're going to be all right," the voice murmured. The voice sounded far away. She'd heard it before.

"No," Jennie heard herself cry. She had to fight it, but couldn't remember why. Jennie struggled against the man who held her. Struggled against the fear and nausea. "No . . ." she whimpered. "Daddy, don't let them hurt me." Jennie leaned her head against the man's chest and gave in to the swirling darkness.

15

Jennie fought against waking. An awareness from somewhere in her brain told her she didn't want to wake up. Her head hurt and her mouth felt dry and sticky. Scenes from her jumbled dreams resurfaced. Ryan lying on the cave floor, bleeding. She'd been running, trying to get away, falling. Terrified.

She tried to think—tried to separate dream from reality. The late afternoon sun poured its honeyed light through Gram's windows. The radio alarm beside Gram's bed read six o'clock. She'd slept all day. Maybe longer.

Someone was playing "Music Box Dancer" on Gram's piano downstairs. Gram? It was her favorite piece. But that didn't make sense. Gram was in the hands of a gang of ruthless criminals, wasn't she? Unless . . . Maybe she had been dreaming.

Jennie liked that idea. It would explain why everything had been so disjointed. If it really was a dream, Gram wouldn't be missing at all. She'd be downstairs right now, playing the piano.

Jennie eased her aching body out of bed and looked down at her rumpled shirt, stained with Ryan's blood, and the loose-fitting jeans rolled up at the hem. Ryan's jeans. Well, that shot the dream theory. You don't change clothes in a dream. Dreams don't cause the skin on your wrist to rub off from the ropes you were tied with. Jennie looked around for her jacket and found it lying across the end of her bed. She reached for it. The lightness of it told her even before she checked the pockets that the gun was gone. *You wouldn't have used it anyway, McGrady,* she reminded herself. That was true, but she'd have felt better knowing it wouldn't be used against her.

As Jennie passed Gram's dresser, the image of a wild-haired, waiflike apparition appeared in the mirror. Her heart slammed against her chest, then settled as she realized it was her own image. She grabbed Gram's brush and pulled her hair into a ponytail.

As she replaced the brush on the dresser, Jennie's gaze strayed to the photo of Gram, Grandpa, and J.B. A fuzzy memory skidded into place. J.B. had been the man at the cave. Jennie picked up the photo J.B. had given Gram and studied his face. He didn't look like the criminal type. *He's Gram's friend,* she told herself. But so was Joe.

Even after all she'd gone through, Jennie felt more curious than afraid. Why had J.B. brought her to Gram's? Where did he fit in? Did he have anything to do with Gram's disappearance or the diamonds? Jennie figured the only way to find out was to ask.

Not smart, McGrady. He's got Dan's gun. And what if he's one of the diamond thieves? It could be a trap.

Somehow Jennie didn't think so. If he had been working with Dan and Joe, wouldn't he have taken her back to the Wakefield house? The fact that she was still alive probably meant she was safe, at least for the present.

Jennie took in a deep breath of what she hoped were both air and courage, and headed for the stairs.

He came into view as she reached the landing. A

broad-shouldered, gray-haired man. Tall. He looked almost like his picture only a little heavier, more wrinkles around the eyes and mouth, and less hair. Jennie watched as he left the piano and lowered himself into Gram's favorite chair.

Jennie took a step forward. His steel-gray eyes met hers. Her bravado slithered away like an old snake skin. *What are you thinking of, McGrady? This man could be dangerous. What if he's the boss, the one Joe and Dan had been talking about?* She was about to turn and run back to Gram's bedroom when he raised his hand and motioned for Jennie to join him.

"Come sit down, lass." As Jennie approached she noticed his eyes had changed from hard granite to a muted ocean gray. "Terribly sorry about the business in the cave this morning, but I thought you and I should have a chat."

"Did you have to knock Ryan out for that? Why didn't you just ask me? I'd have talked to you. And how did you find the cave?"

"Quite by accident, I assure you. I'd taken a walk out on the rocks last evening and saw you and your friend disappear into it. I hadn't intended to involve either of you in my investigation, but realized you might be able to help."

Strange, she thought as she moved toward him. Jennie couldn't explain it, but she wasn't afraid of him. She should have been terrified. Maybe whatever he'd used to put her out had melted a few brain cells. Or maybe it was his accent. He sounded a lot like Grandpa McGrady had, only more English than Irish. Jennie dropped onto the sofa. "Who are you?"

He studied her as though she were an amoeba under a microscope. He smiled again, then leaned back in his

146

chair, stretched out his long legs, and rested his feet on the overstuffed footstool in front of him.

"And what did you do with Ryan?"

"Easy now, lass," he crooned. "Your friend is fine. Didn't mean for him to get hurt . . ." He paused for a moment to stroke his chin. "When I arrived this morning I'm afraid I startled him. He took a swing at me, slipped, and hit his head. I was just about to see to his injury when you got up. Didn't think you'd come with me quietly, particularly after seeing your young friend, so I used a mild tranquilizer. Once you were out I brought you back here, rang the sheriff, and asked him to look after the boy."

"You didn't have to drug me." Jennie hated drugs. The thought of this man injecting her with something without her knowledge or permission infuriated her.

He shifted and cleared his throat. "Look, lassie, that was a minor miscalculation on my part. Didn't know who you were at first . . . only that you'd been staying here. Thought you might be mixed up in Helen's disappearance. I hadn't seen you since you were a wee child. When I brought you back here and saw the photos upstairs, I realized my mistake. I hope you won't be telling your Gram about it. She'd have my hide. At any rate, it was quite a mild sedative," he said, frowning. "Quick-acting and few, if any, side effects."

Jennie considered arguing with him. Drugs were seldom harmless. She also thought about trying to escape, only she kept thinking about the phone message and the picture on Gram's dresser. She didn't think he'd hurt her and figured she was better off asking questions and trying to find out what part he was playing in all this.

"Who are you?" Jennie asked again. "What do you

want? And what have you done with my grandmother?"

"One thing at a time, lass," he said. "First of all, I've not done a thing with your Gram. I've been trying to locate her."

"How do I know you're telling me the truth?" Jennie wanted to believe him. He seemed nice and she had this feeling about him. *You felt that way about Joe too*, she reminded herself. *But you were wrong—almost dead wrong*.

He hesitated, then pushed the footstool aside and leaned toward her. "I don't blame you for being weary of me." He reached into the breast pocket of his suit. Jennie flinched, remembering the missing gun. When he pulled out a wallet and flipped it open, she relaxed again. The flap of his wallet dropped to reveal a badge. "Jason Bradley, Federal Bureau of Investigation. Your grandfather and I worked with British Intelligence—came to the States together."

Jennie shifted her gaze from the badge to his eyes. Maybe it was the way he'd said it, or the sincere expression on his face, but she was beginning to trust him.

"Knew your father as well—named after me, he was. Jason McGrady was a fine young man."

At the mention of her father's name, Jennie melted.

"You really knew Dad? Do you know what happened to him? They worked for you, didn't they? Grandpa and Dad. They were agents."

He nodded. "The best."

She held her breath, wanting, yet not wanting, to know the answer to her next question, afraid the hope rising in her would be crushed again. "My father was working for you when he disappeared, wasn't he? Is . . . is he still alive?"

J.B. stood up and walked to the window. He seemed to study the landscape outside. "We don't know, lass," he finally answered. "There's a possibility."

Jennie pulled in a long, ragged breath.

"Is Gram an agent, too? Are you working on a case? Is that what all this is about?" If Gram was an agent after some international jewel thieves . . .

"No," he said. "Not an agent." He moved away from the window and sat down on the couch beside me. "You're a perceptive young woman. Remind me of your Gram, and your father too. Helen does the occasional odd job for me. Interviews people. Delivers documents—that sort of thing. Nothing too dangerous, mind you. She was running an errand for me in Calgary. When she didn't call in, I made a call to Sheriff Taylor, who told me she'd stayed on in Canada and was working on an article. I wasn't too concerned until Tuesday morning. Someone called my private line asking for her, and I knew something had gone wrong and thought I'd better lend a hand. I've been trying to find your Gram since I arrived yesterday."

"You don't know anything about the diamonds, or the guys who took them?"

"Diamonds? I'm afraid not. As I said, after the phone call . . . but then that was you, wasn't it? Smart girl, cracking that code. Why don't you tell me what you've got and maybe we can work together to find your Gram."

Why not? Jennie was exhausted and more than ready to hand this entire affair over to someone more suited to detective work than she. And J.B. was not only Gram's friend, but an FBI agent.

Jennie told him about Joe, Dan, and their mysterious boss, and how they had kidnapped her so Gram would tell them where she'd hidden the diamonds. By talking it through with him and eliminating the Canada trip and

Gram's dealings with J.B., things started to make sense.

"If I know your Gram," J.B. said, "she's gotten herself involved in exposing this crooked deputy. I suspect she passed herself off as one of them to get into the thick of things."

"And the deal went sour."

J.B. gave Jennie a speculative look. "That's one way to put it. Now, how about showing me those diamonds?"

"If they're still here." Jennie led him upstairs. Once she'd loosened the panel, she let J.B. reach into the wall space. He pulled up the brown paper bag and set it in the floor between them.

"Quite a stash." He lifted up a handful of jewelry and let it fall into the bag again. "Do you have any idea who she might be working with?"

"What do you mean?"

"Helen's too smart to work alone. She'd have at least one contact."

"Like Sheriff Taylor?" Jennie asked.

"Possibly." J.B. closed the sack and started for the stairs. "If I'm not mistaken, the thieves will want the diamonds more than they want Helen. I think it's time to do a little negotiating."

"What are you going to do?"

"I'll talk with Sheriff Taylor. See what he knows about it. If he is her contact, the warrant may have been issued to throw the real thieves off the track and to give her an in. Then we'll see if we can't strike a bargain—your Gram in exchange for the diamonds."

"And once Gram is free, you and the sheriff can move in and arrest them."

Once downstairs, J.B. set the bag of jewels on the dining room table. "We're going to need something stronger to carry these in," he said. "This sack is splitting."

In the utility room off the kitchen, Jennie found a canvas bag. She handed it to J.B. and watched him make the transfer.

J.B. started for the door, then turned back as if he'd changed his mind. "I know you're worried about your Gram, lass, but promise me you'll stay put. These people are dangerous and I don't want you getting hurt. And try not to worry. I'll have your Gram back in no time. And I'll check on that young man of yours as well."

Jennie didn't argue. As much as she wanted to tag along, she'd had enough excitement and adventure to last a decade. This business about being a detective was fine in novels, but in real life? No thanks.

As J.B. disappeared into the woods, she closed her eyes. This had to work. It would work. Gram would come home. They'd go to Florida just as they had planned. "Please be all right, Gram," Jennie whispered. "I love you so much."

16

Needing to do something while she waited, Jennie had some blueberry yogurt and an apple, then headed upstairs to take a shower. Twenty minutes later, feeling refreshed and somewhat human again, she decided to straighten up the house.

She had just started to dust the end table when the phone rang. It was Mom.

"Jennie, thank God I've finally gotten ahold of you. I've been trying to reach you for two days. I kept getting either a busy signal or that obnoxious answering machine. Are you okay? How's Gram?"

Two days. A quick calculation told her that it was Thursday night. *Time sure flies when you're having fun.* Jennie ignored the sarcastic thought. "I'm fine, Mom. I should have called sooner. Things have been kind of hectic around here."

"Are you still sick? I wanted to come down Tuesday, but I had three different clients with IRS audits and couldn't get away. I knew you'd be fine with Gram there, but . . . I like having you home where I can keep an eye on you."

"Mom," Jennie said, "there's something I need to tell you." Jennie felt terrible about lying to her mom, and regardless of the consequences, she needed to make a confession. "I'm not sick." She went on to tell her about Lisa taking her place at camp so Jennie could look for Gram. She wanted to tell her about all the other things that had happened, but not on the phone and not until she had talked with Gram and J.B.

"Mom?" Jennie asked when she'd finished. "Are you still there? Are you mad at me?"

"Jennie, I don't think mad comes anywhere near to describing what I feel right now. I can't believe you'd lie to me like that! I thought we had a good relationship; that I could trust you. And to drag Lisa into it? What were you thinking of?"

"I . . . I'm sorry. It's just that I was so upset about you and Michael, and when Gram didn't come home I knew something was wrong. I had to try to find her."

"I can understand your concern about Gram. But you shouldn't have gone down there alone. You should have talked to me."

"I know. What I did was stupid and dangerous. And I know you'll punish me, but . . . are you going to ground me so I can't go to Florida with Gram? I mean . . . I could understand if you did. I probably deserve a lot worse than that."

"I don't know. At this moment I feel like grounding you for the rest of your life. Jennie, I'm so disappointed. This is absolutely the last thing I'd have expected from you."

Her mom paused. Jennie could hear her draw in a deep breath and let it out. "I won't keep you from going to Florida. That wouldn't be fair to Gram. But I do expect you to continue counseling with Gloria and go to the counseling camp as soon as the Florida trip is over."

"I guess I owe you that, at least." Jennie brushed the rag over the table legs. "Mom?"

"What?"

"I just want you to know I love you."

"I love you too, sweetheart." Mom was getting weepy. "Just promise me you won't ever lie to me again."

"I won't. And Mom? I'm sorry about the way I acted about you and Michael."

"I just wish we could have talked about it." She sniffled. "Well, we can be thankful it's all worked out. You're safe. Gram's back home. Now maybe things can get back to normal."

Gram is home? Why would she say that? Jennie hadn't said anything about Gram being there. "How did you know Gram was back?" Then remembering what she'd said to Lisa about keeping Kate and Mom from coming to the coast, Jennie asked, "Did Lisa tell you?"

"No, Gram called Kate on Tuesday afternoon to let us know she was home."

Of course. They made Gram call so the family wouldn't be worried about Gram or her. They thought Gram had been here all along. Jennie debated whether or not to tell her mom that Gram was still missing, then decided not to. Trying to explain what was going on over the telephone would probably send Mom into a panic attack. Better to wait until Gram came back and the ordeal was over.

"Ah . . . Mom? Let's have a family picnic here at the beach this weekend. That way Gram can celebrate Nick's birthday and everyone can see her. She's been through a lot these last couple of weeks and . . . I just think you and Aunt Kate should . . . you know . . . talk to her and make sure she's okay."

154

"That's a wonderful idea. Kate and I had already talked about one of us going down, but I think your idea is much better. I'll call her and see what we can work out and, one way or the other, we'll see you tomorrow."

After saying goodbye, Jennie attacked the dust again, then moved to the dining room to throw out the paper J.B. had left on the table. It felt good to have her life coming together again.

Jennie crumpled the grocery bag. A couple of newspaper clippings fell out and drifted to the floor. As she dropped to her knees to retrieve them, one of the headlines caught her eye. "1.2 Million in Diamonds Stolen from Trade Show." It was a morning-after account of the robbery. Whoever had pulled off the job, the article said, had to have been an insider with working knowledge of security and alarm systems. That fit Joe all right. The other clipping was an article about Sheriff Taylor's retirement. *Strange. Why would these be in the bag with the diamonds?*

Jennie turned the clippings over and at the end of the story about the diamonds, Gram had written, "Sam's retirement fund . . ." with three question marks after it.

The implications crashed down on her like a truckload of bricks. Sheriff Taylor was behind the diamond heist. Could he have been the "boss" Joe and Dan had mentioned? If that was true, J.B. would be walking straight into a trap. Once Sheriff Taylor had the diamonds, he'd kill Gram and J.B. Then he'd probably come after her and Ryan as well.

Jennie stashed the clippings in Gram's desk, grabbed a sweatshirt from the closet, and headed out the door. She had to stop J.B. before he met up with the sheriff.

As she ran, scenes of the past couple of days flashed

into her mind, the puzzle pieces finally coming together. Sheriff Taylor and his men had stolen the diamonds. For some reason Gram had gotten hold of them and hidden them in her house. They had kidnapped her and had been trying to make her talk. He'd probably issued a phoney warrant so he and Joe could search the house and throw the trail off themselves.

She should have suspected him when he showed up at the Wakefield house, where Joe and Dan had been holding her prisoner. She'd thought he was just making rounds. He'd known she was there all the time. Joe had tried to keep her from seeing Sheriff Taylor that day. Probably following orders. Jennie had seen him, though, and could identify all of them.

Sheriff Taylor had lied about getting a phone call from Gram. He probably forced Gram to call the Johnsons and Kate so they wouldn't be worried and come looking for her. *That was so smart, Gram,* Jennie thought. *By calling the Johnsons instead of us on Nick's birthday, you tried to let us know you were in trouble. Too bad it took so long to figure it out.* Jennie realized now that she should have talked to Mom and Kate and Uncle Kevin about her suspicions rather than trying to handle it on her own. If she had, maybe she wouldn't have been kidnapped, Gram might be safe now, and Ryan . . . Jennie prayed that the sheriff didn't know how much Ryan knew about the case.

J.B. had about a forty-minute head start, and Jennie wasn't sure where he had gone. Since Joe and Dan had taken her to the Wakefield house, she decided to head there first. The setting sun cast a deep red glow across the sky. In a few minutes it would be completely dark.

As she approached the long driveway leading to the house, a car turned in the drive. Its headlights illuminated the woods, and Jennie dove off the trail and scrambled behind a rock. The gravel crunched as the black Cadillac headed toward the house.

The engine stopped. Two car doors slammed. "Get her inside," a man's voice ordered. It might have been Sheriff Taylor, but Jennie couldn't be sure. She moved out of her hiding place and inched closer. The car's dome light spotlighted Dan as he opened the back door of the car and hauled out a woman's body.

17

Gram is dead. The message slammed into Jennie's brain. *No! She can't be. Be rational about this, McGrady. If she was dead, they wouldn't have brought her here. Would they?* Jennie moved closer. Dan and Joe were only about twenty feet away, and if either of them looked this way they might see her, but she had to know.

As Dan hoisted Gram to his shoulder, she groaned in protest. Jennie let go of the breath she'd been holding and sank to her knees.

The two men entered the house. Joe turned briefly to close the door and stopped. He nearly filled the doorway, blocking the light from the house. He stepped back out on the weathered gray wooden porch and looked around. Had he seen her?

Jennie curled into a tight ball, expecting him to come thrashing into the bushes after her, but he didn't.

"Joe." Sheriff Taylor joined him on the porch. "Do you see something out here or are you having second thoughts?"

"Thought I heard something," Joe shrugged. "Probably a squirrel."

The men turned to reenter the house. The sheriff stopped on the threshold and looked back. His eyes met hers. At least she thought they did. Light bathed his face and silvered hair. A chill shuddered through her. He looked like he always had—kind, honest, law-abiding. He'd been the sheriff of Bay Village for over twenty years. People trusted him. Jennie wondered what had happened to make him turn to crime.

Sheriff Taylor disappeared inside and closed the door. Jennie unfolded herself from her cramped position behind the bush and jogged toward the house.

Don't do it, McGrady, a voice in her head warned. *Go for help. You don't have a chance against three armed men.* She had J.B., she reasoned. Going back to Gram's to call for back-up would have been the logical thing to do, but there wasn't time. Besides, who would she call? The only people Jennie trusted were Ryan and J.B. Unfortunately, she had no idea where they were and hoped the sheriff hadn't already gotten to them.

She tried not to think about that as she crept up on the porch and inched her way to a large bay window. The living room was dark except for the glow cast by the room beyond it, probably from the dining room or kitchen. Sheer drapes clouded her vision, but she could see well enough to know that no one was in the room.

Rather than go past the front door, Jennie climbed over the porch railing and made her way around to the back where the window's light cast a square-shaped spotlight on a weed-infested plot that had probably once been a garden. She grabbed the ledge and pulled herself up. Jennie peered into the kitchen and then into the room beyond, seeing four men hunched over the dining room table. She recognized Sheriff Taylor, Dan, and Joe, but the fourth was partially blocked by the kitchen wall. She had to get a closer look. The table sat directly in front of another large bay window. She moved toward it, past the kitchen door, past the garbage cans.

"Yowl!" One of the garbage cans clattered to the concrete slab that extended from the kitchen steps. A black shadow streaked past her. Jennie whipped around the corner just as the back door opened. She pressed against the house, willing her body to disappear into it.

"Who's there?"

"What's going on?" The voices belonged to Joe and Dan.

The black cat, apparently feeling repentant, chose that moment to make amends. He curled around Jennie's legs and purred. Jennie stooped to pick him up, and the eerie feeling of *deja vu* washed over. She saw the black boots, the jeans . . . only this time the hand was holding a gun.

Jennie started to scream. Joe clamped his hand over her mouth.

"Shhh," he whispered. "I'm not going to hurt you." Joe slowly removed his hand and holstered the gun. "You're lucky it was me. Dan would just as soon kill you as look at you. Give me the cat and get out of here."

"But . . ."

"Go. Before Dan shows up."

That was all the incentive Jennie needed. She ran for the trees and dove behind a bush just as Dan rounded the opposite corner.

"Just a cat." Joe held the animal up for Dan to see, then lowered it to the ground. It scampered away and headed straight for Jennie.

"Meow."

"With friends like you . . ." she murmured, scooping the cat into her arms as she watched Joe and Dan go back into the house. She stood there for several minutes, stroking the silky fur and wondering what had happened. Why had Joe let her go? Was he Gram's contact? Had he been working undercover to expose Sheriff Taylor? Or was he just one of those crooks who didn't mind stealing, as long as no one got hurt.

Jennie wanted to believe in Joe. She wanted to believe that her intuition had been right all along, but she couldn't take the chance. Gram's life and maybe even J.B.'s and Ryan's were at stake, and Jennie had to find a way to save her. First, though, she needed to discover the identity of the fourth man.

She set the cat down. "Go home," Jennie whispered, giving him a shove. He ran a few feet then looked back. "Go." Jennie lunged at him and he scampered off.

A large maple blocked Jennie's view of the dining room window where the men had been seated. She ran for the tree and flattened herself against it. Through a set of sheers that matched the curtains in the living room, Jennie could see the men's shadows. The curtains kept her from seeing them clearly, but they also served as protection against them seeing her.

Jennie crept the rest of the distance to the house. She stopped at the window, inched forward and peered in.

Her heart dropped to the vicinity of her feet. Her throat tightened. J.B. was sitting at the table; a satisfied grin stretched across his face. He wasn't making a deal with the crooks. He was one of them. J.B. lifted his hand high above the center of the table. A shower of glittery diamonds dangled from his hand. Sheriff Taylor grabbed them and laughed.

"I'll have to admit, I didn't think you could pull it off J.B. Getting the McGrady girl to talk was sheer magic."

161

"Yeah," Dan added, patting his holster. "I appreciate you getting my gun back too. Felt kind of naked without it."

Jennie thought she was going to be sick. J.B. had used her. She felt as though some invisible hand were squeezing her heart. She wasn't certain whether she was more angry at him or herself. She had trusted him. Trusted her intuition. And she'd been wrong again.

Sheriff Taylor pushed his chair back. "I'd say this calls for a toast, gentlemen. I'll get us some drinks. Dan, you'd better check on our guests." He gestured upstairs.

Guests? Sheriff Taylor must have brought Ryan there from the cave. J.B. had been in on it all along. Oh, he was slick. She'd believed everything . . . his story about working with Grandpa, Gram, and Dad. . . . How could she have been so stupid?

Pull yourself together, McGrady. You don't have time to think about how J.B. betrayed you. Gram and Ryan need help—now. Jennie brushed the tears from her cheeks. She had to figure out how to get into the house and up to the second floor. If she could get inside maybe she could release Gram and Ryan, and they could all get away. Then they'd call the police and let them deal with the crooks. A good plan. And, from her vantage point, it looked as if all she had to do was flap her arms and fly.

Taking cover behind the maple, Jennie looked for a more traditional route to get inside. The tree's branches nearly touched the house but weren't big enough to hold her. Except for one. A main branch connected with the roof of a closed-in porch. The porch, only one story high, stretched beneath two bedroom windows. Maybe she could get into one of them. She jumped to the lowest branch, caught it, and swung up. From there it was easy, one branch, then the next.

In less than a minute she'd reached the porch roof. The first window was open a crack, just enough to get her fingers under it. She braced herself and pulled. Nothing. She pulled again and realized the window had been painted shut and nothing short of a sledge hammer was going to dislodge it.

"C'mon, McGrady," she muttered, trying to give herself a pep talk. *Don't give up. Maybe the next window.* When it wouldn't open, she sat down on the moss-covered shingles and buried her head in her arms. *There has to be a way in. There just has to be.* She looked up at the stars and sighed. "You got any bright ideas?"

Jennie sat there a few minutes, feeling the moisture soak into the seat of her jeans. A toilet flushed and the light in a window to her right went out. The bathroom! She'd opened the window when Joe had untied her long enough to use the toilet.

By stretching, and plastering herself against the house, she could stand on the porch and get hold of the bathroom window sill. With one hand she pushed the window frame up as far as it would go. It still looked too narrow, but it would have to do. Jennie shifted to get a better hold. Her foot slipped. Her hands, acting on pure instinct, closed over the sill. She swung up and sideways, trying to get back to the porch roof. The wet moss, slippery as a patch of ice, denied her a foothold.

Jennie figured she had two options. One was to let go and fall the fifteen or so feet to the ground and risk breaking her neck. The other was to climb. Jennie opted for the second and prayed she'd have enough strength in her arms to make it.

18

By hooking one elbow, then the other, over the windowsill, Jennie gained enough leverage to pull herself up and poke her head through the window. Then her chest. For the first time since junior high, Jennie was glad she didn't have much cleavage to brag of. Lisa would never have made it through there.

Lisa wouldn't be crazy enough to try.

She'd gotten about halfway in when she heard footsteps in the hall. *Don't come in . . . please don't come in.* When she heard the heavy footfall on the stairs she started breathing again.

Jennie managed to crawl the rest of the way in, hoping her entrance didn't sound like a thunderstorm to anyone but her. Once inside, she crept down the hall to the bedroom where Joe and Dan had kept her. The streetlamp provided barely enough light to see the lumpy dark form of a human body stretched across the full length of the bed. Jennie eased forward, leaned against the bed, and turned the body over. Ryan.

She pulled off the gag and untied his arms and feet. "What . . ."

"Shhh. It's me," Jennie whispered. "Are you okay?"

Ryan sat up and rubbed his wrists. "I . . . I think

so." He touched the bruise on his forehead and winced. "Got a heck of a headache though."

"Can you walk?"

Ryan swung his legs over the edge of the bed and stood. "I'm not sure." He swayed and sank back onto the bed, pulling Jennie down with him. She put an arm around his back to keep him propped up.

"What's going on?" His voice was slurred.

Jennie told him what had happened at the cave and after. "I'll fill you in on the details later, but right now we've got to find Gram and get out of here."

This time when Ryan stood, he seemed stronger but still had to lean against her for support. Gram was in the bedroom across the hall. Jennie rushed forward and undid her gag while Ryan loosened her hands and feet.

"Jennifer Kathleen McGrady," she whispered, "what in the name of heaven are you doing here?" They wrapped their arms around each other. She'd lost weight, Jennie noticed, but she was alive and strong enough—she hoped—to escape.

"You shouldn't be here," Gram reprimanded her, still keeping a loose hold on her granddaughter's shoulders.

"I had to come. I couldn't let them kill you. Sheriff Taylor, Joe Adams, Dan, and a guy named J.B. are downstairs right now. They have the diamonds." As quickly as she could, Jennie told Gram and Ryan that she'd given the diamonds to J.B. and then found the newspaper clippings. "I came to warn J.B. about Sheriff Taylor, then realized he was in on it too. I'm so sorry, Gram. I thought J.B. was your friend. I trusted him. And he's as big a crook as the others."

"You were right to trust him, Jennie. If he's won Sam Taylor over we're as good as rescued. Joe's on our side too. He's been working undercover . . . trying to keep us safe and to get enough evidence on Sam and Dan to convict them. With me having the diamonds that's been hard to do."

Her explanation was interrupted by footsteps on the stairs. "Quick, into the closet—both of you. Stay out of sight."

"But . . ."

"Go!" Gram quickly twisted the ropes back around her feet and hands.

Ryan still looked dazed, so Jennie grabbed his hand and pulled him into the closet just as the bedroom door burst open. She watched through the narrow slit between the hinges.

Sheriff Taylor stepped up to the bed, holding one of the diamond bracelets in Gram's face. "Looks like we won't be needing you to tell us where the diamonds are after all. Your friend here couldn't resist my offer." He laughed. "Too bad he won't be able to enjoy his share."

"Mr. Bradley . . ." Sheriff Taylor lifted his gun from its holster and pointed it at J.B. "Have a seat next to Helen." He turned and shoved the gun into Joe's side. "Hand over your gun, Joe. Nice and slow. That's it. Now, sit on the bed with the others. Move!"

"What's this all about?" Joe lowered himself to the bed on the other side of Gram.

"Did you really think you two could pass yourselves off as crooks?" Sheriff Taylor snorted and shook his head.

Jennie leaned back against Ryan for support. His arms went around her. They were going to die. All of them. When Sheriff Taylor and Dan shot Gram, J.B., and Joe, she would scream or cry, and they'd know she and Ryan were there. The sheriff would kill them too.

166

Get a grip, McGrady. You won't cry. You'll handle it. No. You won't have to handle it because it's not going to happen. You won't let it happen. You're going to come up with a plan.

Right. A plan. Create a diversion. Yes. That could work. It did in the movies. She'd wait for the right moment, then do something that would distract Sheriff Taylor and Dan so the others could get a jump on them. Jennie pressed her face against the door frame to watch for the right moment.

Sheriff Taylor lifted a hand to stroke Gram's cheek. "We would have made a great team, you and I." He sounded sad, wistful, as though he really cared about her. "You could have been a wealthy woman, Helen. I'd have taken right good care of you. But you couldn't be satisfied sharing it with me. You had to have it all." He stepped back beside Dan.

"Sam," Gram shook her head. "Don't do this. Give yourself up before it's too late."

He laughed. "It's already too late. You shouldn't have taken the diamonds. In a way, I'm glad you double-crossed me. It makes what I have to do easier. It won't be hard to explain having to shoot you. You being a thief and all."

"I didn't double-cross you. You know that. I took the diamonds so I could return them to their owners and talk you out of this nonsense. We've been friends for years, and I couldn't stand by and see you destroy your life."

Sam laughed. "What life did I have to look forward to? Retirement on a $800-a-month pension? That's barely enough to pay the rent."

"I had hoped I could reason with you," Gram said. "But you've changed, Sam. You've become as greedy and

167

ruthless as the criminals you helped put behind bars."

"Maybe," Sam said. "But I'm a whole lot smarter. The way I figure it, these two officers cornered you and you shot them, but not before one of them shot you. The tragedy of it all was that when you died, the location of the diamonds died with you. I'll retire as planned— maybe head on down to Mexico. Dan," he beckoned to the man behind him, "let's get this over with."

"My pleasure," Dan said as he lifted his gun from its shoulder holster and aimed it at Gram's head.

"No!" Jennie screamed and threw open the door. The room exploded with gunfire.

Ryan yanked her to the floor and fell on top of her. Joe staggered against the wall as a bullet ripped into his shoulder.

Gram leapt at Dan, kicking him hard in the groin and knocking the gun out of his hand. He groaned and doubled over. J.B. punched Sheriff Taylor so hard he collapsed against the wall and sank to the floor.

It was over. Ryan rolled away and Jennie sat up. The whole thing had been so unreal, she half-expected a movie director to bounce in and yell, "Cut. It's a wrap. Great job everyone. Jennie, D-a-w-ling, you were spec-tac-ular." And they'd all laugh and go home and everything would be like it was before.

But it wasn't a movie.

J.B. and Joe had Sheriff Taylor and Dan sprawled out, belly-down on the floor, while they searched them for weapons and slapped handcuffs on them. The closet door had taken the bullet meant for Ryan and her. The splintered hole was as big as a baseball.

"Are you children okay?" Gram pulled Ryan and Jennie into a three-way hug.

Jennie opened her mouth to answer, but nothing came out. Now she knew what it felt like to be scared speechless . . . or was that spitless. Either way worked for her.

Gram lowered her arms and got that I-think-you-and-I-better-have-a-talk look on her face. It was going to be a long night. The look was replaced by one of concern as her gaze shifted from Jennie to the men. "Joe, you're bleeding."

Jennie spun around, remembering that he'd been shot. Aiming his gun at the sheriff and Dan, Joe held his left hand tight against his right shoulder. Blood had leaked from the gunshot wound onto his shirt and between his fingers. "J.B., how about . . . giving me a hand with these two. I think . . ." he winced, "you'd better drive. Helen . . . I'll need your statement just as soon as you can get to the courthouse. Jennie . . . Ryan, you too . . ." Joe's voice trailed off and he buckled.

J.B., Gram, Ryan, and Jennie all moved at the same time. Jennie got to him first.

She placed her fingers alongside his neck, the way she'd been taught in the Red Cross first aid training class, and pressed her other hand against the wound. "His pulse is still okay, but we'd better stop the bleeding." Ryan pulled off his shirt and helped make a compress. J.B. tended the prisoners while Gram went downstairs to call 911. Minutes later sirens pierced the air.

Between getting Joe to the hospital, taking the prisoners in, and giving their statements, it was three hours before the police in Lincoln City released them. Before heading home they stopped back by the hospital to see Joe. He was in surgery. The doctor had assured them that after he removed the bullet and repaired some muscle and tendon damage, Joe would be fine.

It was after midnight by the time they got back to Gram's. They were all so tired they could hardly stand. J.B. said he was going to his hotel room to sleep for two days. Gram said she was taking a long bath and planned to sleep for a month, then added, "I'll see you in the morning."

"Want some hot chocolate or something?" Jennie asked Ryan after Gram had gone upstairs.

"Not really," he said, falling back on the couch. "I think I'm too tired to lift the cup."

Jennie sat next to him, leaned her head against the cushioned sofa back, and closed her eyes. She felt a little deflated—like a balloon gone flat. Glad they had made it through—glad it was over. But somehow she wasn't ready for it to end.

"You were great tonight," Ryan said.

Jennie turned her head and looked at him. "Spec-tac-ular." She laughed and added, "You were pretty great yourself."

He squeezed her hand. "Want to go agate hunting tomorrow?"

"Love to." She smiled and closed her eyes again. *Tomorrow.* All of a sudden she loved that word. She had come too close to losing all of her tomorrows.

Tomorrow morning Gram and Jennie would sit down at the kitchen table, or on the patio overlooking the ocean if it was nice, and talk about the case. Gram would lecture her about the dangers of sleuthing and then she'd hug her and feed her blueberry pancakes and bacon and peppermint tea.

Tomorrow they would go to the hospital again to see Joe—they'd take him some flowers and tell him how wonderful he was.

Tomorrow Ryan and she would hunt for agates and shells and play tag in the surf. And he would kiss her and tell her he loved her . . . maybe.

And tomorrow she would see Mom and Nick . . . and Michael . . . and Aunt Kate, Uncle Kevin, Lisa, and Kirk. Tomorrow her family would all be together again. And Gram would be with them. She'd tell the whole story like she did when she came back from Mexico, and no one will believe her—except Jennie, Ryan, and maybe Lisa.

Jennie glanced over at Ryan. He'd fallen asleep. She lifted his feet onto the couch, tucked a pillow under his head, and covered him with a light blanket. After turning out the lights she headed upstairs, past Gram's room, to the spare bedroom.

It didn't take long to get ready for bed. She said her prayers, realizing that God had answered most of hers in the last few days and had kept them all safe. In a way, he'd also answered her prayers about Michael and Mom. It was up to Jennie to set the date for their wedding. She wondered what they'd say if she told them to wait until the end of summer . . . if she told them she wanted to find Dad first.

Maybe this was God's way of giving her more time to find him. Hope swelled inside her again. "Thank you, God," she said. "For everything."

Before turning out the light, Jennie had one more thing to do. She pulled her journal out of her pack and began to write.

Dear Dad,

You'll never believe what happened. I solved my first mystery . . . okay so I had some help. It was scary—no, make that terrifying. I thought we were all going to die.

171

You should have seen me, Dad. I hung in there like a true McGrady.

I'm going to talk Gram into looking for you, but with Joe in the hospital and J.B. visiting and everyone coming down this weekend I don't know when I'll get the chance.

I will though . . . you can count on it.

I'll love you forever.

Jennie

Jennie turned off the light and thought about flying to Florida. Maybe they'd be somewhere over the Rockies when she would turn to Gram and say, "Gram, I've been thinking about Dad . . ."